D

Cake

A Bakery Detectives Cozy Mystery

By

Stacey Alabaster

Table of Contents

Introduction 1

Chapter 1 2

Chapter 2 12

Chapter 3 23

Chapter 4 39

Chapter 5 49

Chapter 6 67

Chapter 7 81

Chapter 8..106

Chapter 9..121

Chapter 10 138

Chapter 11 148

Chapter 12 159

Epilogue...165

Introduction

Thank you so much for buying my book. I am excited to share my stories with you and hope that you are just as thrilled to read them.

If you would like to know about all my new releases and have the opportunity to get free books, make sure you sign up for our Cozy Mystery Newsletter.

FairfieldPublishing.com/cozy-newsletter

Stacey Alabaster

Chapter 1

Belldale, Summer Time

"Are you ready for your close-up, Rach?"

"Huh?" I asked, leaning closer to the camera. "I thought this was just a test run! I haven't even got my makeup on yet! Don't tell me this is actually going to go to air?"

"Relax," Justin, the producer of *Baking Warriors*, said as he rolled his eyes at me. "I'm just teasing you. We'll shoot the proper intros tomorrow. This is just to test the lighting."

I let out a sigh of relief. Not only was my make-up not 'reality TV star ready', I hadn't even memorized the script. Yes, reality shows have a script. And even though I hadn't been officially cast yet, I still had to shoot the dreaded intro shot where I gave my name, age, and some pithy quote about how the other contestants needed to watch out for me and my supreme baking talents.

Justin ushered me away from the cameras and placed his arm around my shoulders. "Rach," he whispered, "about the age thing."

I stopped. "About what age thing?"

He peered at me through his thick-rimmed glasses with his hand perched on his hips. "Your age thing. We're thinking...instead of saying that you're twenty-six, we go with twenty-two. Hmm?" He looked me up and down. "You could just about pass. For a 'TV' twenty-two anyway. Not in real life."

I just stared at him. "Twenty-six is old now?"

Justin shrugged. "Twenty-two just sounds better, doesn't it?" He waved his hand. "That way we can showcase you as the young contestant, the wunderkind that runs her own bakery at just twenty-two." He glanced down at his tablet like it held more interesting content to him than the conversation. "After all, twenty-six is not all that impressive, is it?"

I thought it was. And if he really wanted some kind of interesting angle to my on-screen personality, well, there were always the recent murders I had solved. For just a second I considered telling him everything, but there was a reason I had left out my history as an amateur sleuth when I'd auditioned. I had to remember that was not what I wanted to be known for if I did end up being cast on the show. "Why not just shave off a few more years then? Why don't we just tell the viewers I'm eighteen, go all the way with it?"

Justin glanced up from his tablet. "Oh, honey, we've got to be realistic here."

I'd only sent in my audition tape to *Baking Warriors* on my best friend Pippa's insistence last year. When I hadn't heard anything back eight months later, I'd totally forgotten about it. Then I got the call: the show was doing 'round the country auditions for its fourth season and they were coming to Belldale to film an audition episode. Of course, the producers had already whittled down the auditionee list to a final ten but they were still putting on the pretense of an open cattle-call style audition the following day, where any amateur baker in Belldale could come along and 'audition' to be on the show.

"You'll be here at 5:00 AM tomorrow, right?" Justin called out to me, temporarily removing the earpiece that I thought was a permanent addition to his head.

I nodded. "5:00 AM. I really need to get out of here now though." I stopped, my hand poised on the studio door as Justin listened to something in his earpiece. He held his hand up, a sign that I was to stay put.

"We just need to do one last test."

"Justin!" I double-checked the time on my phone. Yep, I was already late. Pippa was going to kill me if I left her stranded. "I really, really have to go."

He ushered me back over to chair. "We must leave nothing to chance. Trust me, honey, it is my neck on the line here."

I sat back in my chair and groaned inwardly. Was the chance of becoming a reality TV star really worth all this hassle? We hadn't even started shooting yet—heck, I hadn't even gotten *cast* yet—and it had already taken over my life.

I sat there for a few minutes then jumped to my feet. "All right, is that it?" I grabbed my purse and ran for the door before Justin even had the chance to look at me again, let along drag me back to that chair.

"5:00 AM!" I heard him calling through the swinging doors as I bolted for my car. "5:00 AM, Rachael, and not a moment later!"

***

"The 10:10 flight from Oregon has been delayed."

Groans came from the arrivals lounge. Personally, I couldn't decide whether I was relieved or annoyed. A small delay I would have been pleased with, as I was already twenty minutes late, but an hour's delay? I kept looking at the time, trying to figure out how much sleep I could get before my call time. "If the flight gets in at 11:10, and it takes twenty minutes for Pippa to find her luggage, and it takes an hour to drive back to Belldale, and Pippa and I take a half-hour catching up, and I need a half-hour to get ready in the morning, and there's a forty-five minute drive to the studio..."

Great, that was about two and a half hours of sleep.

I tapped my foot nervously as I waited for the check-in list to finally light up yellow over the delayed flight's name to show that the plane from Oregon had touched down. I wasn't even sure why I was so nervous. I was acting more like I was waiting for a long lost lover than a long lost best friend. It was just that Pippa always had a habit of surprising me.

But in her last email, she had promised me that there were no great shocks awaiting me when she stepped off the plane. "Honestly, Rach, no new piercings, no crazy new hair style. I'm not pregnant and I haven't adopted a kid! I've just had a nice, boring vacation chasing paranormal entities."

Well, we would see about that. There were plenty of things that she could have left off that list.

But her not having any big news suited me at that moment because I couldn't *wait* to tell her about *Baking Warriors*. I'd managed to keep the news of the audition quiet, even though Pippa had always told me she'd kill me if I ever kept a secret from her.

She was going to practically wet herself when she heard the news. I'd been reluctant to even audition, but Pippa was convinced that I would make the perfect contestant on her second favorite television show, behind Criminal Point.

I wanted to see her face when I finally told her.

I just hoped she wasn't going to shock me before I had a chance to surprise her.

***

"Miss." An elbow dug into my side. "Flight's here."

I sat up and apologized for falling asleep on the strange guy's shoulder. "Don't worry about it," he said as I zipped up my jacket, sinking into it as I tried to hide my reddening face. I glanced at the time on the arrivals list. At least I'd managed to sneak in an extra half-hour's sleep.

Everyone pushed and jostled for position as I tried to spot Pippa in the crowd. She'd promised no crazy hairstyles but I'd seen her most recent photos and knew her present hair color was purple. In Pippa's world, though, that is not crazy. That is normal. Crazy for her would be, like...shaving an obscene word into an otherwise baldhead, or something. I hoped she hadn't done that. Especially if she was going to work at my bakery while I was away shooting the show.

There she was. The wild lavender hair made her stand out in the crowd.

But she was not alone as she walked, practically skipped, up the long hall of the arrival's lounge. I tried to push to get to her, but the crowd was too thick and I ended up with a sharp heel in my foot as a lady with a large bouffant stepped back on me.

I guess I'll wait my turn then.

"Who is that?" I whispered, looking at the handsome stranger walking far too close to Pippa. "Please tell me it's just someone she met on the plane, a new friend." They moved closer to each other and Pippa had a gross love-struck look on her face. "Oh no, don't do that!" I said as the man reached for Pippa's hand and gripped it in his before giving it a kiss.

They remained linked like that until they reached me, standing there with an expression that was frozen into a wide-eyed grin.

Pippa turned her grin towards me and started bouncing up and down. "Rach," she said, sucking in a breath of excitement. "Don't get mad at me, okay, but I have a little surprise for you." She turned back towards the mysterious stranger and started bouncing higher.

"*Who is this*?" I asked through gritted teeth, though I was still smiling. I tried not to panic.

"This," Pippa said dramatically, like she was about to announce the winner of a reality show competition, "is Marcello!" She dropped his hand and shoved hers in my face, pointing to a gigantic bauble on her ring finger.

"Rach!" she said, jumping up and down. "We got married!"

"W...what?"

She shoved the ring further into my face. Yep. It was a ring.

"When...when did this happen?"

Pippa snuggled into this so-called Marcello, who reached for my hand and kissed it. "It is wonderful to meet you," he said with an accent I couldn't quite place.

I gulped. "You too. Pippa...can I just...have a quick word with you."

"Wait here for a moment, sweetheart," Pippa said to Marcello before smothering his face with kisses. "Just a bit of girl talk."

I ushered her off to the side.

"What is it?"

"Pippa, how long have you know him?" I whispered.

"Oh, Rach, it doesn't matter how long we've known each other! It only matters how in love we are!"

"How long?"

Pippa looked sheepish. "Three weeks."

"Pippa!"

She looked up at me and pouted. "Aren't you happy for me?"

I sighed. "Yes," I said, reaching over to give her a hug. "I just can't believe my best friend got married without even telling me!" I leaned back and gave her a playful hit with my purse. "I wasn't even invited!"

Pippa shrugged as she moved back towards Marcello, like he was a magnet and she was a big piece of metal. "Don't worry, we haven't had the reception yet. I'm planning a big party in Belldale next week!" Snuggled under Marcello's arm, she turned back to me and asked, "You don't have anything big going on next week, do you?"

"Umm, actually..."

Chapter 2

Summertime had taken all of Belldale into its warm embrace. People were, in general, jollier at this time of year, the sun and heat making them lazier and less likely to stress out.

And less likely to commit murder. Belldale had been at peace for almost six months. No strange activity, no paranormal sightings, and no unexplained deaths.

It would almost have been boring if we weren't all in such cheerful moods. Summer was a good time of year for the hospitality business and everyone on our little food strip was doing very well, especially my shop, "Rachael's Boutique Bakery."

Which was why I was hesitant to leave it behind to go shoot a TV program for three months.

"I'll be fine! Of course you can leave me in charge!" Pippa squealed after I told her the news back in my apartment. "Rachael, there's no way you are missing this opportunity." She squealed again and clapped her hands.

"Okay, okay," I said, giggling a little. "Calm down though, I haven't made it through the final audition yet."

"Oh, you will though!" Pippa grabbed my hands and started jumping up and down. She was clearly still on a post-nuptial high. And I had to admit her newly rejuvenated enthusiasm for life was rubbing off on me, even though I was still skeptical about the stranger who was waiting in the next room.

"Where is he going to...fit?" I whispered, peering out the door. All I could see was the back of Marcello's head, all dark curls.

Pippa shrugged. "He's just going to have to snuggle up on the sofa with me!"

"Right..."

It wasn't the right time to have a talk about her maybe finding her own place and moving out, though I knew that moment would have to come.

I heard something breaking in the kitchen. "Oh," Pippa said, making a face. "Sorry about that. He's a little clumsy. But that's all part of his charm." She patted me on the arm. "You'll get used to it. After all, we're going to get very cozy, the three of us living here together!"

I took a deep breath and smiled at her. "Yes, we are."

There was another crashing sound, followed by a loud, "Sorry about that!"

I wondered how much sleep I was actually going to get.

***

"Honey. You look terrible. Straight into makeup. That should take care of most of it." Justin shoved me towards a makeshift tent that was brimming with men and women in black shirts holding panels of powders and bronzers and looking even less awake then I was.

"Remember, we want her looking twenty-two!"

It was a long morning. And I mean LONG. When it was finally time for me to scurry my way past the line of hopefuls that thought they actually had a chance of making it onto the show, I felt like I was going to keel over. Two hours was the amount of sleep I'd gotten the night before. And right then I was running on caffeine and Justin's barked orders.

"Now," he said, brushing my hair off my shoulder and examining my face in his hands. "Do you remember what you have to tell the judges?"

I nodded groggily. "I'm twenty...two..."

Justin nodded. "What else."

"I own my own bakery. Baking has been my passion since I was a little girl. I baked my first cake when I was only three..."

Justin let out a long sigh.

"What?" I asked, a little offended.

"It's just not very exciting, is it?" He waved his hand in the direction of the crowd that lay outside the studio. "I mean, that might pass for excitement in this place, but it just doesn't make for very compelling TV, does it, darling?" Another sigh. "Are you sure there's nothing else interesting about you, honey?" He looked upwards and clucked his tongue. "Maybe we can make something up. Did you parents die when you were very young?"

"No!" I said. "And I'm not going to pretend they did. It's gotta be bad karma or something."

"Well, we have to think of something quick." He dared a look inside the judge's room. "Something that's going to impress them."

"What about my baking?" I asked, as though that should be the obvious answer. "I thought I was supposed to impress them with my super skills in the kitchen. Isn't that kind of the point of the show?"

Justin laid a hand on my shoulder and shook his head slowly. "Oh, sweetie, you really have no idea how this TV thing works, do you?" He consulted a list on his tablet. "Maybe you're a lost cause. One of these other guys might have an interesting back story...maybe something tragic in their past that we can get them to open up about."

"Wait!" I placed a hand on top of his tablet. "I do have an interesting sort of hobby," I said reluctantly.

There was a slight glimmer of interest in Justin's eyes. "Go on."

I took a deep breath and quickly told him everything that had happened in Belldale over the past year: the three deaths, the paranormal mysteries, and my part in solving the cases.

Justin's jaw was wide open by the time I'd finished. "Now, why didn't you lead with that?" He placed a gentle hand on my shoulder and guided me to the judging room before lowering his voice. "I had no idea this town was so interesting. Huh. I've only been here a couple of days and I almost died of boredom."

"Yeah, well, it's definitely not boring all the time."

He raised an eyebrow. "I guess I just came at the wrong time of year then."

I shifted uncomfortably. "Things have been peaceful here recently. I don't want to jinx it. Besides..." I trailed off, a little reluctant to continue.

"Besides what?"

I shrugged. "All the deaths and stuff kind of gave the town a bad rap. I don't think certain members of the police department would like me bringing all that stuff up on national TV."

I could see the glimmer in Justin's eyes growing stronger. "Oh, honey," he said. "What 'certain members'? A man, I take it." He shot me a knowing look. "One that you dated, maybe?"

"No," I said quickly, wrapping my arms across my chest. "I just want to respect their wishes."

Justin nodded. "Don't worry, honey, I understand. We won't sensationalize anything." Then, into his walkie-talkie, he announced my audition number and name to the judges. "Up next we've got, Rachael. Belldale's very own number one Murder Expert!"

"Justin!"

***

17

There were three of them.

I tried to focus on the "nice" judge, a blonde lady named Dawn who was late middle-aged. She was known for giving the contestants constructive, rather than downright vicious, critiques. And I tried to ignore the glares of Pierre, the judge who was known for giving no holds barred criticism and occasionally reducing contestants to tears with his caustic barbs. Not that it dulled his popularity. Of the three judges, he was by far the most famous and the most beloved on social media.

Then there was Wendy. Nobody really paid much attention to her.

"Go on, dear, tell us a little about yourself," Dawn encouraged. "What is all this stuff about murders we've been hearing so much about?"

"I, erm..." I caught Justin's glare out of the corner of my eye. "Don't stammer," he had told me.

"Why don't you try one of my cakes?"

I turned around to fetch the cakes I'd prepared the day before but which the producers made to look like I'd baked that day. I knew the judges had already tasted them the day before and made up their minds, but we had to go through the motions.

"Delicious," Wendy said, pushing her long dark hair out of her face. "Wouldn't change a thing, darling!"

A nice, but fairly hollow—and, let's face it, useless— comment.

I focused on Pierre, who screwed his face up as he slowly chewed the chocolate cake I had presented him with. I wondered why he had to make such a show of it when he already knew what it tasted like and already knew what he was going to say.

He finally placed his napkin down and swallowed. Then he stared straight at me for a good ten seconds before he finally delivered his verdict.

"That was...fine," he said. Nonplussed. No expression on his face except a dead stare. "Tell me, Rachael, why you deserve to be on *Baking Warriors* over the thousands of auditionee outside?"

The nine other auditionees, I thought. But with his stare on me, I was in no state to be smart with him. Or even to defend myself.

"I...I...um, I've been baking since I was three years old," I said rather meekly. "It's...it is my passion...."

Pierre leaned back and shook his head. I saw his gesture for a producer, then heard him whisper, "Can we use any of the murder stuff?"

Justin shrugged. "If she gets through." He shot me a look over his shoulder then returned to Pierre. "Though I really don't think she will. Shall I bring in the next contestant?"

Pierre nodded. "I've had enough of this one."

"Thank you for you time," I said softly before Justin led me swiftly out of the room and told me to return to the green room. I didn't even get to hear Dawn's verdict.

I was red-faced and annoyed by the time Justin finally joined me for a debrief. He just shrugged. "It's dog eat dog, honey. You should have led with the murder stuff."

I sat down on a soggy sofa. "I'd rather not get through than use any of that stuff." I was aware that I was acting sulky but it had been a long day and I just wanted to go home. "I don't know why I'm still here. I obviously didn't get in."

Justin sighed and looked down on me in pity. "Look," he said. "Just between you and me, you've still got a shot. A good shot. Look, I do NOT say this to everyone..." He lowered his voice. "But you are going through to the next round. Just sit tight and relax. You look good on camera and the judges really liked your cakes. That's all there is to it."

I looked up at him in shock. "But Pierre didn't seem impressed at all!"

Justin waved his hand dismissively. "Oh, that's all just for TV, honey. Pierre's the executive producer. If he likes you, you'll go through. Just relax. Have something to drink." He fetched a bottle of wine from the cooler.

"No, thanks. I'm afraid if I drink I'll fall asleep."

"Come on, just a little sip! Honey, you'll have to start drinking if you get into TV."

I reluctantly accepted half a glass.

Just as Justin was plugging the cork back into the bottle a high-pitched squeal sounded from the direction of the judging room.

Justin let out a loud, exaggerated sigh that said, "I don't get paid enough for this." He threw the wine bottle back in the cooler. "Probably a rejected contestant. Or a judge who hasn't got their lunch on time. Wait here while I deal with it. I won't be a minute."

But Justin was way longer than a minute. After ten minutes had passed and Justin hadn't returned, I started to get worried.

Then I saw the ambulance.

"Are you okay?" I said, running towards a stricken-looking Justin with his headpiece in his hands. "What on earth has happened?"

Justin, white as a sheet, slowly looked over his shoulder and, with a trembling voice, simply said, "Pierre's dead, Rachael. Somebody killed him."

Chapter 3

"I'm just asking, Pippa. It's a simple question. WHY does he lose so much hair? Where does it even come from? He wasn't even in the house today."

Pippa put her hands up in a shrug that said 'I have no idea why Marcello molts like a llama, but gosh isn't he so cute for doing so?'

Which, I mean...sure. If you're in love. But I wasn't in love with the guy. I was just the girl who ran around after him with a vacuum cleaner twenty-four hours a day.

"I'm sorry, Rach. I'll vacuum more." Pippa plunked herself down and let out a deep sigh of contentment. "Isn't he just the greatest?"

Ermmm. "Yes. The greatest."

Pippa folded her legs underneath her so that I could squeeze onto the sofa next to her. "We're not taking up too much space, are we?"

Well, I was currently squeezed up onto the tiny sofa that doubled as her and Marcello's bed and I couldn't move around the apartment without banging into one of them. But I forced a grin. Pippa was happy. That was all that mattered at the moment. "No. It's fine."

"You'll let me know if it gets to be too much, won't you?"

I was just about to reassure her that I would when we both heard another smashing sound from the kitchen. Pippa started to giggle, making another 'isn't he just so cute' expression. "He has this thing," she said, laughing so hard that she could barely get the words out. "Where he tries to place an item down on the bench—like a knife, or a cup, or a plate, you know, whatever—but he totally misjudges where the end of the bench is! So it ends up on the floor!" Now totally full of mirth, Pippa threw her head back in throes of laughter.

I just stared at her. "Is that thing called bad eyesight?"

Pippa just started laughing even harder. She even slapped her knee. "No, Rachael! It's just one of his cute, little, quirky things."

Yeah, it was pretty cute and quirky that he was breaking everything I owned. I sighed myself. I had bigger things to worry about anyway.

Marcello appeared with a bowl of chips for us and placed them down on the coffee table with an apology. "I broke the jar of salsa. I'd better go finish cleaning that up." He paused. "Unless you want me to scoop the salsa up and pick the glass out, and I can bring that in for you?"

"No," I said quickly. "Thank you, that's fine."

He disappeared into the kitchen again and I just shot Pippa a look of disbelief. Even she was making a face at the suggestion of eating glass-shard-filled salsa that had been scraped off the kitchen floor.

Remind me to never offer him a job at my bakery.

He'd apparently been job-hunting that day. I shuddered at the thought of the sorry soul who'd have to employ him.

I picked up a chip and stared at it sadly. So this was what it had come to. Ever since I'd been diagnosed with a *severe* allergy to gluten, I'd basically had to switch from sweet snacks to savory. For a baker, it was almost a fate worse than death.

Pippa seemed to read my mind. About the death thing, that is, as she crammed a chip into her mouth and started to talk with a mouth full of crunchy potato. "So what are you going to do?"

I placed my chip back down and leaned back against the sofa. "Nothing, Pips. This isn't my circus. It's not my monkey."

She just stared at me. "It very well IS. Rachael, you were practically cast on that show before that guy went and died! You can't tell me you're just going to sit back and do nothing! What happens if they delay filming entirely? Or worse, redo all the auditions."

"Yes, that's the great tragedy of today, Pippa. Not the poor dead guy. The poor dead guy who was poisoned, by the way."

"You know what I mean." Pippa sat up and grabbed my arm. "You're the PERFECT person so solve this murder, Rachael!" She held up her fingers as she listed off the reasons. "One, you were there. You probably met the killer. It's got to be a fellow baker, right? Two, you can't let this opportunity slip through your fingers. Where else are you going to get a chance to become a reality TV star?" Then she got to the item she clearly considered the most important of the lot. "Three, you have plenty of experience in this area. I can't believe you're not already out there interviewing suspects."

I huddled up against the back of the sofa and muttered to myself.

"What was that?" Pippa said, leaning closer to me.

"Jackson doesn't want me interfering anymore, okay?"

Pippa opened her eyes wide. "Since when has that ever stopped you before?"

Pippa had been gone for over six months, so I didn't blame her for not understanding my change in attitude regarding sticking my nose in police business. But a lot had chanced in Belldale over the last six months. With two high profile murder investigations, the entire town had changed in character. It had become more withdrawn, somehow darker and less open.

"With *Baking Warriors* coming to town, I think Jackson—all of us, actually—hoped the town could be seen in a more positive light," I tried to explain.

"Well, that hope was short lived." Pippa threw another chip into her mouth and raised her eyebrow.

"Yes, but an amateur sleuth sticking her nose in this, one who might be about to become a minor celebrity no less, is not a good look for the police department. They are trying to revamp their image. Jackson wants them to appear more competent. To assure the town that they can keep them safe. I should just keep my distance."

Pippa gave me a long skeptical look that made me squirm. "Rach, I keep hearing a lot of 'Jackson wants' coming out of your mouth. What do YOU want? Why do you even care what he thinks anyway? Hasn't he gone and shacked up with that skinny detective with the red hair?"

Detective Emma Crawford. Yes.

"I don't care about that," I said unconvincingly.

"Sure sounds like it."

I sat and thought for a moment. Why *was* I so happy to keep my nose out of the investigation? Even though my feet *were* kind of itching to get into the fray, and I had to keep trying to stop my mind from racing— thinking over all the events of the day, trying to figure out who had access to Pierre, who was close enough to him to poison him, and who had a motive to do such a thing.

The truth was, I didn't *want* to see Jackson. So when he'd asked me—politely, mind you—to keep my nose out of cases, I hadn't really minded. I didn't mind keeping my distance from him one bit. He was happy with another woman now. And I was fine with that. Just fine. I hadn't seen him in months.

There was another smashing sound from the kitchen.

I leaned back against the sofa and closed my eyes while Pippa laughed hysterically. "I think we might owe you a new set of dishes by now."

Maybe I needed to invest in some headphones.

***

"What...the..."

The entrance to the road where my bakery stood, Pillock Avenue, was totally blocked off by vans and people racing around with boom mikes and cameras.

"What's going on?" Pippa asked from the passenger side.

"It looks like they are filming *Baking Warriors* here or something," I said, which was the only thing that made sense to me in that moment. Because that's what the swarm of people and cameras and producers wearing earpieces running around reminded me of filming on the show.

"Well, can we get through? Should we let them know that we actually work on this street?"

It was still early in the morning, 6:30 or so, and even though we had a hot day ahead of us, the fog and dew from overnight caused a smog to appear over the street. So it took me several minutes to realize that it wasn't the *Baking Warriors* film crew at all, but was, in fact, several dozen separate film crews, all with different garish logos plastered on the side of their vans.

"OH," I said, sucking in my breath. "Pippa, they're news crews."

"Oh," she said warily, leaning forward to see if there might be any space where we could fit the car through. I already knew there wasn't.

"I guess news of Pierre's death has broken," I murmured.

Pippa spun back to me. "Of course it has. Did you really think people wouldn't find out that a beloved celebrity has been killed? Did you not think that people would be incredibly interested to find out what happened to him?"

I turned the ignition off and groaned a little. "I don't know. I thought the police had ways of keeping this sort of thing quiet for a little while. Or at least controlling the media presence a little."

In the time we'd been sitting there, even more vans had pulled up to join the circus, more tents pitched, and even more vats of coffee set up.

So much for Jackson's plan to keep the town out of the spotlight.

So much for his plan to make the town feel safer.

I checked the time on the dash. We were going to be late to open.

"Let me see what I can do," Pippa said, pushing her door open. I picked up my phone and used it to quickly scroll through the day's news.

Yep. Pierre Hamilton's death was the biggest breaking story in the entire country. It was the featured story on countless local and national news websites.

This was not going to be a good look for Belldale.

I glanced up to see Pippa arguing with a reporter in a blue suit who had hair that looked too grey for his fresh looking face. I rolled down my window so I could hear what was going on. He was shaking his head at her before he threw up his hands and shouted, "I don't know what to tell you! I'm not in charge of this whole thing! Us moving our van isn't going to make much of a difference."

Pippa turned in a huff to a different reporter, a smiley looking blond woman whose smile died as soon as the news camera turned off. She scowled at Pippa and told her to get out of the way.

"Out of your way?" Pippa exclaimed. "You're the one in our way! We actually live in this town! We work on this street. And we need to get past!"

I almost jumped out of my skin when I heard a tapping on my window.

"Jackson," I gasped. It was the first time I'd laid eyes on him in what had to have been three months. During that time, I had managed to not only avoid solving crimes, I'd also managed to avoid seeing him. So I was doing well.

He looked different. Slimmer, I think it was. Or maybe his hair was longer. It seemed to sit up on his head in more of a bouffant than the last time I'd seen him. And was it my imagination or was it a little grayer than the last time I had seen him?

"Rachael?" he asked, and I jumped again as he interrupted my thoughts.

"Um, hi," I said, straightening up. I self-consciously reached up and touched my hair, wondering if the professional styling I'd received before filming yesterday was still holding up under the damp of the soggy morning. "How are you?" I asked stupidly, not really knowing what else to say.

"Well," Jackson said with a raise of his eyebrows as he shoved his hands into his pockets, his badge dangling down the front of his torso. "As you can imagine, busy."

I nodded. "We went so long without a murder too, bit of a shame." Another stupid thing to say. I was nervous. I didn't know what was escaping my mouth. I stared at the steering wheel while Jackson fidgeted back and forth on his heels.

"I heard that you were there when it happened."

"Nearby," I corrected him. "In a different room."

"Hmm."

I kept staring at the steering wheel. Another murder in Belldale happening while I was less than a hundred feet away. There had been talk for a while—from Pippa mostly, who doesn't always have her feet firmly planted in reality—that I was cursed. Silly, right?

I wasn't so sure.

"Do you need me to answer any questions?" I asked quietly.

"We'll take a statement later," Jackson replied quickly. I took note of the 'we,' not an 'I.' That meant he'd be sending some uniformed officer to ask questions, not himself.

There was that distance again.

Jackson cleared his throat. "It's good to see you again anyway, Rachael."

"Is it?" I asked.

He looked away. "Let me see if I can clear this road for you."

He stomped away towards the hoards of vans and reporters like a man on a mission. Waving his badge like a sword, he was quickly able to part the sea of cars and news crews. Pippa came sprinting back to the car, breathless from arguing with people. "I almost got punched!" she exclaimed, pulling the door shut quickly. "Rach, some of these people are VICIOUS."

I eyed them slowly as we finally managed to pull the car through the crowd. "I'm sure they are."

"Why are they all staring at us?" Pippa whispered, slumping into her seat so that she was almost on the floor of the car.

"Maybe because you were out there trying to fight them two minutes ago?"

But I wasn't so sure that was the reason. They didn't seem to be staring at Pippa.

They seemed to be staring at me.

***

My new baker-come-assistant-manager Bronson had matters well in hand by the time we finally got to the bakery. I heaved a heavy sigh of relief as I pulled the door open and was hit by the sweet smell of breads and cakes baking.

Bronson emerged from the kitchen covered in flour. "I figured you'd have issues getting here on time this morning. I rode my bike," he explained, wiping his hands on a tea towel, which he then flung over his shoulder. "Pippa!" he exclaimed as she followed in behind me. "Welcome back!"

Pippa grinned and ran up to him with her left hand outstretched.

"You're kidding me," he said, mouth agape as he took in the rock on her finger. "Who is the lucky man?"

Don't ask, I thought as I walked around to the cash register to check that we had enough change for the day. The bank was at the end of the street, and I didn't like our chances of getting through that crowd unscathed again.

Pippa continued to rattle off a list of Marcello's plethora of charms while I counted the change in the till. We didn't have enough. We had almost none in fact. And I doubted that our customers were all going to pay for five-dollar desserts with credit cards. I was about to interrupt the other two to check if either of them had any change I could use, when my phone started to flash with a call.

Justin.

I frowned and wondered whether I should answer it or not. After all, the whole reality show casting thing was all on hiatus now...wasn't it?

It would be stupid of me to think he was calling to tell me that I got on the show. Obviously that's not his priority right now, I told myself.

But what if it is about the show and my place on it, and I don't answer his call?

I pressed 'accept.'

"Rachael?" His voice sounded hurried and desperate, not that unusual for Justin, but it was missing its usual air of superiority mixed in.

"That's my name, don't wear it out." Boy, I was really saying some dumb stuff that day.

"Rachael, where are you right now?"

"At work," I said flatly. "Where else would I be?"

"You work?" He sounded momentarily flummoxed.

"Yes. As a baker! You know that!"

"Oh." Justin paused. "I thought that was just made up for the TV show. You're an actual baker?" He let out a little surprised sound. "Most of the time, the people on the show can't even bake, they just get cast because they're good for TV and then we put them through a two week intensive course to bring them up to speed. Otherwise, we just get someone else to bake the stuff for them." I could practically hear his disaffected shrug from the other end of the line. It hadn't taken him long to go from desperate sounding to dismissive.

"Justin, why are you calling me?"

He seemed to remember and the desperation returned to his voice. "You've got to leave work. You've got to come here immediately."

"I can't just leave work." I stared out the window and sighed. "Literally. I'm trapped here. But even if I wasn't, I can't just up and leave."

"Rachael, I need your help."

He always needed something from me, but usually it involved me sitting in a makeup chair for hours or memorizing an asinine script. Something told me this was a completely different matter, though. "Why, Justin?" I instinctively lowered my voice so that Pippa and Bronson couldn't hear me. "What's going on? Where are you?" I turned so that my back was to the others. Pippa is a pretty good lip reader. Luckily, she still hadn't grown tired of talking about how great Marcello was.

"I'm in my hotel room," he whispered, as though he also had someone waiting nearby on his end that he didn't want overhearing the conversation. "I'm hiding."

"What are you hiding from?" I whispered back.

"Take your pick," he whispered, exasperation entering his voice. "The press, the production crew, the police." He gulped. "Rachael, they think I did it."

Chapter 4

"Hey, where are you going?" Pippa turned, the jingle of the door giving me away before I could escape.

"I have to go get some change. For the register."

Pippa stomped over to the window. "But the press are blocking the bank." She looked me up and down. "Besides, they didn't seem to like you."

"Yeah? What was that about? Anyway, I'm sure they'll make some room. I just really need to get to the bank." I tried to push past her.

"Hold up." Pippa stared at me sternly. "I recognize that look on your face." Her eyes went wide. "You're going off to investigate."

"Shh," I said, checking to see if Bronson was overhearing us. "I am not. I'm going to the bank."

"Ohhh, shoot," Pippa said, pointing out the window. "Your boyfriend's on his way over."

"Who?" I looked to see Jackson striding towards the bakery. "Very funny, Pippa. Don't call him that." I undid my coat buttons, suddenly feeling hot and flustered. I'd blame it on the sun that was rapidly rising and melting away the dew if anyone asked.

He at least did the courtesy of knocking on the door, even though Pippa and I were both frozen there in the window like statutes.

"Detective. I wasn't expecting you."

"I did tell you one of us would be by to take a statement." Jackson glanced down at Pippa and asked if he could speak to me alone.

"Sure, I guess."

"Do you have somewhere else more important to be?" There was no hint of humor or amusement in his voice. I glanced at Pippa for help.

"No," Pippa said. "She was just heading to the bank. Isn't that right, Rach?"

"Right," I muttered. "Nothing more important than that. Why don't we go sit in my office then?"

Ever since I'd expanded the bakery by purchasing the shop next door, I'd been able to spread out a little more. The extra space meant a big kitchen, larger cool room, more space for stock, and even a little room for an office. Not that it looked like an office per se, it was really just a desk cluttered with unopened bills and unwashed coffee cups with a mini fridge shoved next to it. The whole thing was really no bigger than a cabinet, if I was honest.

"Sorry," I said, trying to shove the piles of bills to one side as I quickly hid the dirty cups. "It's a bit messy in here."

Jackson glanced up at the ceiling and nodded. "It's good to see you've expanded, though. You never had an office before. Next step will be to franchise out."

"Not quite up to that point yet," I said, sitting down. I was surprised by how casual and friendly he was suddenly being, compared to how serious he'd been in front of Pippa.

My phone flashed. A text from Justin.

Where are you???

I quickly turned the screen face down. Time to get this interview over with, quickly.

Jackson didn't seem to be in any hurry to get to the point, however. He was twiddling his thumbs and shifting in his seat, trying to get into a more comfortable position. I didn't blame him. It was plastic and from the thrift store. Still.

"I didn't see anything," I volunteered, hoping that might move things along more quickly.

Jackson frowned. "Well, that's not a very good start, unfortunately."

I supposed it wasn't, but he was confusing me. From my experience—and I had a lot of it—the cops usually do most of the questioning in these situations. But it was me that had to ask Jackson what exactly was going on.

That's when I saw it. The faintest of eye rolls and a look on his face as though he'd rather be anywhere else, asking anyone anything else other than what he was about to ask me.

Suddenly, I got it.

But I wanted to hear him say it.

"Rachael," he started to say, every syllable dripping with reluctance. "This has to stay quiet, you understand? Unofficial."

"What does?" I still needed to know what he was 'unofficially' asking me.

Jackson swallowed. "Any...involvement, of yourself. In this case."

I opened my eyes wide, acting like I was shocked by the proposition. "You want me to be involved in the case?"

"As I said. Unofficially."

I leaned back in my seat. I could barely control the satisfaction emanating from me. "Well, well, well. This is a first." I leaned forward and stared at him, a little more serious now. "Does anyone else at the station know that you are asking me this?"

Perhaps it was going to be our little secret.

"Emma does," Jackson replied. "Detective Crawford," he added, in case I was confused about who he was referring to. I wasn't. "It was actually her suggestion."

Oh.

I was feeling slightly less satisfied. "I will have to think about it."

Jackson looked surprised. Not just surprised. Disappointed. "You seemed pretty happy about it a second ago."

Even with the screen face down against the desk, I could see it flashing every couple of minutes with a new text. I had to go see Justin.

Jackson didn't need to know that I was already investigating the case. In that moment, I didn't want to give him the satisfaction of saying yes. Especially when it had been his girlfriend's suggestion. I mean, I knew it was petty, but in my opinion, he was being petty as well—even pointing out that it was Emma's suggestion. Couldn't he at least have pretended that he was on board with the scheme?

I stood up and pulled on my coat. Big mistake. The mercury was already rising. It was hot in that cramped office even in just a blouse, let alone a heavy coat. But I needed to show Jackson that I needed to leave.

"I'll have to think about it," I said.

Jackson stood up after me. "What is there to think about?"

I shrugged. "I don't know if I want to get involved in all this stuff again. Especially with my reality TV career about to start."

Jackson just stared at me. "Is this really what this is about? You care more about being famous than helping us catch a killer? You care more about your image than justice?"

I placed my hands on my hips. He wasn't right, of course—I was lying—but I didn't like his self-righteous indignation considering I was pretty sure I knew why he was there. "It's a bit rich to accuse me of caring more about image than justice when there's only one reason you're here, begging me for my help."

"I'm not begging!"

"And that reason is that you are concerned about the image of the police force. Especially with yet ANOTHER killer running around." I waited for him to dare to argue with that.

He let out a little scoff. "And you think that you running around solving this crime is GOOD for our image? If I really cared about any of that, why would I be asking you for help?"

"Secretly asking me," I pointed out. "Unofficially."

His neck seemed to tense up. "Like I said, it's not a good look."

Fine. So he was happy to ask for my help as long as no one knew about it. "And if I solve the crime?" I asked. "I suppose all the credit goes to you."

Jackson rolled his eyes just slightly again. "Solve the crime? No one is expecting you to do that. We just thought you might be able to offer a few crumbs of help, considering you were at the audition yesterday."

"You know what?" I asked, sweating in my red coat now but unwilling to take it off. "I have thought about it. And my answer is no."

Jackson's mouth dropped open as I pushed past him.

"Now, you'll have to excuse me. I've got some important business to attend to."

***

As soon as Pippa and I were back in the car, I yanked my coat off and cranked up the air conditioner. "Geez it's like a heat wave."

"It is when you're wearing a winter coat." Pippa looked me up and down. "Now, are you going to tell me where we're going?"

I glanced in my rearview mirror waiting until Jackson became the size of an ant. "We are going to talk to Justin."

"Who is Justin again?"

"The producer of *Baking Warriors*." I still had my eyes trained on the rearview mirror. "He was the one who discovered Pierre's body."

"I knew it!" Pippa gasped, slapping her hands together. "I knew you were going to investigate!"

I turned to face her. Deadly serious. "Not a word of this to Jackson, understand? In fact, not a word of it to anyone." I leaned back in my seat. "All I'm doing is talking to Justin. I can't make any promises about what will happen after that."

But Pippa wasn't listening to me, she was already bouncing up and down in her seat with excitement. "I thought life back here in Belldale might be boring after my travel adventures. Especially now that I'm old and married."

My eyes widened.

"But investigating the death of a reality show judge?" Pippa shook her head. "Rach, this is far from boring."

"Just stay calm, Pippa," I tried to say. "I can't guarantee anything."

"Come on, Rach. You KNOW you're gonna do it."

I sighed and looked at her.

"Pippa," I said. "If I take on this case, and I do mean IF, will you help me?"

"Are you kidding me?" she exclaimed. "The bakery detectives, back together? Just try and stop me."

Chapter 5

"Wow, this place is pretty flashy," Pippa murmured as we stood in front of the Glassview Hotel. "I didn't even know Belldale had a place like this."

"I don't think production spares any expense," I said. "On the crew at least." I'd already had a sneak preview of the dormitory I'd be sleeping in if I actually got selected to go on the show. I'd be sharing a room with another contestant, and a bathroom with another four. At least during the first weeks of shooting. If I managed to remain until the end, the herd would thin out a bit and I might get my own room.

But it was nice to see that Justin was staying in luxury.

"Who is it?" he whispered from the other side of the door.

"It's me, Rachael. Who do you think it is?"

He yanked the door open. "It took you long enough." He stopped when he saw Pippa standing next to me. "Who is this?"

"This is my best friend, Pippa. She helps me when I do this sort of stuff."

Justin sighed and made a show of looking down both sides of the corridor. "People have been after me all day." He pulled us both inside the room and double-checked the door was locked before heading over to the mini bar.

"Vodka," he announced once he'd found what he was looking for. He didn't offer me or Pippa anything as he took a drink from the tiny bottle. I supposed they were expensive. "Believe me, honey, I need to drink after the twenty-four hours I've had."

"Justin, are you going to tell me what's going on? You said that you were a suspect, but you're not being held at the police station."

Justin began pacing back and forth across the carpet. "No, but I am being held prisoner in this hotel room." He stopped and stared at me. "The press are all pointing their fingers at me, Rachael." He walked over and shook me by the shoulders. "You gotta help me. I know that you're an expert at this kind of thing. You solve murder cases." He flung his arms up in the air. "Well, you gotta solve this one! You gotta help me prove that I didn't do it, otherwise my career is over."

I shot Pippa a look and settled into a chair. "And of course you want justice to be served... You want your good friend Pierre's murder to be solved."

Justin waved his hand. "Yeah, yeah."

Pippa was staring back at me. I couldn't read her mind, but I could read the look of suspicion on her face. She seemed to be saying to me, *But how do we know Justin DIDN'T do it?*

I gave her a slight shrug. *I know.*

If anything, Justin would have been at the top of my list of suspects. He was the one who found Pierre's body. Clearly, the media had leapt to the same conclusions.

And I didn't want to do that. Jump to conclusions, that is.

"Justin," I said gently. "Calm down for a moment. Take a seat."

He gulped down the rest of his vodka and took a seat at a table by the window overlooking the lake.

I stood and joined him. "Take a few deep breaths." Sitting down, I asked him, "Now, do you have any idea who MIGHT have done it."

Justin began to bite the nail of his left thumb. After a few seconds of deep thought, he nodded. "Really, it could have been anyone who was there that day."

Of course.

"But I'm pretty sure..." Justin glanced up at me. "And don't take offense to this, Rachael."

I leaned back. "I won't."

"But I'm pretty sure it was an auditionee."

I gave him a long stare. "Do you think I did it?"

Justin shook his head. "No, no. Of course not. You were in the green room, after all."

I sighed. "Who then? Do you have any names?"

"Wait here a second." He went and fetched his beloved tablet from the top of his bed. I tried not to groan at the sight of that thing.

It took him a few minutes to find the auditionee list.

"Here," he said, sliding it in front of me. "Here is a list of all the potential contestants who got up close and personal with Pierre yesterday."

I leaned over. "Why are some of the names highlighted in pink?"

Justin raised his eyebrows. "They are the people who acted the most suspicious. Rachael, I had to deal with the whole bunch of you all week, you know. Put up with everyone's tears and tantrums, assure you all you were doing all right, that your hair and makeup looked fine, and that you were definitely going to wow the judges."

Not exactly how I remembered events. Anyway.

"So, I saw everyone. Saw their best, and worst." Justin sat down and stared at me. "I know how desperate some of these people were to get on TV." He didn't break the stare. "Desperate enough to kill."

I felt a little chill go down my spine.

He pushed the tablet closer to me. "There you go, Rachael. Those names in pink. They are the people you need to be talking to."

***

Justin had narrowed the list down to two prime suspects. The first one was a woman named Renee, a struggling single mother with five kids under twelve who would have been an almost certainty to make it onto the show—unless someone else had a better backstory than her.

I was worried that person might have been me.

Justin had told me that Renee was desperate for the $100,000 prize money. She'd talked about little else during the pre-audition phase, apparently.

"Pretty good motivation," I said to Pippa as we stood in the front of Renee's house. I glanced guiltily at the front of her house. It looked like the money really *could* come in handy. The house wasn't just a little rundown. It would take more than just a fresh coat of paint to get this place looking nice. Or even livable. There were planks of wood falling off the exterior and the porch groaned as we stepped on it. I was afraid I was going to fall right through it.

I knocked on the door.

A woman, looking nothing like I was expecting, pulled the door back. "Sorry," I said. "I was looking for Renee Austin?"

"I'm Renee," she said.

"Oh." I stared at the young, perfectly dressed woman in front of me. I tried my best to hide my confusion. I certainly didn't want to be rude, but I desperately wanted to ask how the heck she was so young--or looked so young at least--with so many kids.

And how did she afford to dress so well if she was apparently so desperate to win the prize money? She wore a crisp floral dress in pink and green and her hair was pulled back with a matching headband. She looked the picture of the perfect homemaker. Not someone struggling to put food on the table.

"Can we come in?" I asked, still trying to hide my look of surprise.

"Who are you?"

That was a good question. I should have led with that. "My name is Rachael Robinson."

I saw her face change. Not that it had been soft, exactly, but now her mouth formed into a hard line. "Right. The contestant that beat me to get onto the show. I see."

I didn't know that was official yet. Had I really gotten onto the show?

Right. Not the right time to focus on that.

"What are you doing here? Come to rub my nose in it, have you?"

I shook my head and put my hands up. "No, of course not."

I've just come to accuse you of killing someone.

Probably best not to say it quite like that.

"What then?"

I cleared my throat. "I'm sure you've heard about Pierre's death," I said, trying to be delicate.

Renee raised her eyebrows. "I've heard that he was murdered, yes. On set, apparently."

"Yes. Apparently." I turned to Pippa, begging her silently for help.

"Erm," she said, turning towards Renee. "You didn't happen to see anything suspicious yesterday, did you?"

Renee lowered her eyes. "What is it to either of you two? I've already spoken to the police. Why are you at my house?"

I decided to just be honest with her. "Look. The police in this town don't always do the best job when it comes to things like this. Sometimes they need a little...help. So that's all I'm trying to do. I'm concerned—just like you are, I'm sure—about what happened to Pierre. What does it mean for our town?" I decided to try a slightly different tactic. "What does it mean for the future of the show? I'm sure you're anxious to find out whether you got on."

"What does it matter whether Pierre is alive or dead? I blew the audition."

"Hey, I thought I did too," I said, trying to be sympathetic. "But Justin assured me that I didn't. Apparently I did better than I thought I did."

Renee scoffed. "There was no 'apparently' about it. Everyone knew you were getting through. Everyone knew you were Pierre's little favorite," she said with a hiss before trying to shut the door on us.

Pippa shot me a *look*.

What is going on here?

"Renee, please, if you could just let us talk to you for a minute! Pierre didn't even seem to like me! He didn't even like my baking that much."

She shut the door with my foot caught between it and that doorframe. "Ouch!"

"I'm sure your baking wasn't the reason he liked you!"

I yanked my foot out before it got jammed again, before Renee slammed the door for good.

"What was all that about?" Pippa asked, clearly enthralled by the drama but trying to look sympathetic for my sake.

"I think my foot is broken." I tried to flex my toes and winced. "And I have no idea what all that was about. That was crazy, right?"

"Had you met her before?"

I shook my head. "This was the first time I ever laid eyes on the woman. I never even heard of her until this morning."

"Well, it seems like she knows an awful lot about you."

"Pippa," I said, slightly offended. "Whatever she was just suggesting, and I'm not even sure what that was, none of it is true. You know that, right?"

Pippa shrugged. "Hey, if you had to flirt with a judge to get onto a reality show, then I don't blame you."

"Pippa! I didn't. I only met Pierre the one time, at my audition. And I was so nervous I could hardly even speak to him. Let alone flirt."

The curtains to the front porch pulled back to reveal Renee's face scowling at us.

"Right. We should probably get off her porch."

***

"So who's next on the list?" I asked as I pulled out of Renee's driveway. She was still peering at us through the curtains as I rolled my car slowly backwards.

Pippa frowned and looked down at the names. "Some guy named Adam Ali."

"Adam Ali," I murmured, glad to finally be out of Renee's crossfire. "Man, that name sounds familiar. I really hope it's not who I think it is."

***

It was. Adam Ali was a thirty-five year old man, claiming to be twenty-five, who was convinced that he had been robbed of a life in show business. He had ginger hair that had been highlighted blonde, pale skin, and blue eyes that were far too bright.

It had been *years* since our last meeting.

I knew him because he owned a wedding cake business. When I'd first opened my boutique bakery, he'd tried everything possible to get me shut down, including getting other shop owners and residents to sign a petition that alleged that my bakery sold goods containing illegal substances and that I was a hazard to the family-friendly neighborhood.

Eventually, when I'd informed him that I didn't even *make* wedding cakes and never intended to, he backed off.

Still, I knew just how competitive, and underhanded, Adam could be. No wonder Justin had him pegged as a suspect. I could only imagine the lengths he would go to in order to ensure his place on TV.

"Pippa, Adam isn't going to just open up and talk to us. He probably isn't even going to let us in his shop." I turned off the ignition and thought. "We're going to have to come up with a good reason for going in there."

Pippa held up her left hand. "Duh?" she said, pointing to it.

"Oh, Pippa, you're a genius! Your reception!" I threw my head back. "Oh, I'm almost glad you actually got married now!"

"What?"

"Huh? Nothing," I said quickly, taking my seatbelt off. "I mean, of course I'm glad you got married. As long as you're happy, I'm happy."

"Right."

"Come on, let's go inside!"

Adam's face bloomed into a large grin as soon as he saw Pippa and the ring on her finger. "Don't worry, there's a wedding band as well, as you can see, but we haven't had the reception yet!"

I lingered back out of sight and almost got trapped in a large display of taffeta decorations falling from the sky.

I tripped over a display and almost sent a very expensive four-tier cake flying.

"You!" Adam said, his mouth dropping open. He raced over and straightened the display, shooing me away. "Have you come here to sabotage my store?"

"No, I wouldn't stoop to that level," I said, gripping my purse straps as I tried to steady myself on my feet. "I'm here with my friend Pippa."

"Oh, you two are friends?" His disappointment was palpable.

Pippa nodded. "Yes, best friends. Rachael would have been my maid of honor as well, if me and Marcello hadn't eloped."

Adam shot me a skeptical look before placing his hand on his hip. "So are you two actually here to buy a wedding cake?"

Pippa nodded. "Yes, of course!" A look of shock spread across her face when she flipped over a price tag and saw the price.

"They aren't cheap, honey, but they are the best." Adam turned to me pointedly and added, "I am the best baker in Belldale, after all."

I tried not to bite. I really did. "Is that so? Then why did I get cast on *Baking Warriors*, and you didn't then, Adam?"

Adam's mouth dropped open. "You auditioned for *Baking Warriors*?"

Huh? "Oh, come on, Adam, don't pretend you don't know I was there. Or that I was the judges' favorite."

Adam pouted a little and crossed his arms. "I *didn't* know you were there, actually. The least you could have done was stay away and give me my moment! After you opened up the only other rival boutique cake shop in town and took away all my customers!"

I rolled my eyes. "I don't even do wedding cakes. My store has nothing to do with weddings at all."

I could tell immediately from his reaction that I'd said the wrong thing. "Oh really, Rachael Robinson? Is that so?"

I was less sure now. "Yes?"

Adam clicked his tongue in his cheek. "What is all this I've been hearing about you holding wedding receptions then? Do you not cater those? With cakes?"

I looked at Pippa for help, but all she offered was a shrug with a 'you're on your own here' look.

I swallowed. "Well, yes, but that's only a recent thing. And I just hold the receptions. It's not just wedding receptions we do, it's birthdays, bar mitzvahs, and other celebrations," I said, stumbling over my words as I tried to paint the situation in a more positive light. "I think a lot of the brides and grooms bring *your* cakes in to my store actually. They must know yours are the best." I had no idea if that was true. Nor did I have any idea if Adam was buying any of this. I doubted he was.

"Well," Adam said, with a little flick of his bangs. "Mine are the best." Okay, maybe he was. I had to remember, flattery was the way to this man's heart.

"Adam," I said, pouncing on the fact that his guard was down a little. "I suppose you heard about what happened to Pierre yesterday?"

"Yes, sweetheart, I was there." He stared at me. "I heard the screams." He turned his attention back to one of his cake displays, fixing a ribbon tied around a thick slab of fondant. "Though I've been avoiding all social media today. I can't bear to read about any of it." He placed his hand up to his heart. "It's such a tragedy, isn't it?"

"Yes, it is." I tried to read Adam's tone while he was talking, but it was impossible to tell if he was sincere or not.

"Adam, did you see anything yesterday? Hear anything? Besides the screams."

"Who are you? The police? No. All I heard was the screams of that PA that found him."

"Producer," I corrected him. "Justin is a producer, not a PA."

"Well, whatever. I didn't see anything before or after that. I was more focused on myself." Big shock. "And my own audition, than on anything anyone else was doing."

I thought about this. "Did you think your audition went well?"

Adam glared at me. "I know I gave the best audition of anyone there. I'm sure I would have gone through to the next round as well, but I'm not sure we'll ever know now, will we?" Adam flicked his bangs again, sadly. "Who knows if the show will even film now? It's a tragedy. I was made for TV, Rachael. I just can't believe all of this is happening."

Adam looked over at Pippa. "So are you going to purchase one of those or not?"

Pippa backed away awkwardly. "I'm going to have to think about it, but I'm honesty really very interested."

She kept backing away until she was right at the door. I bid farewell to Adam and quickly followed her out.

"YOU'RE going to bake my wedding cake, right?" Pippa whispered to me as we ran past the shop front.

"Pippa, I've never made a wedding cake before!" I said, opening the car door. "But yes. I will." I shot one last look back at Adam's shop. "I wouldn't trust anything that had been made by Adam."

It was midday and the sun was glaring down. Even with the air conditioning on full blast, we were sticking to the seats. But with the windows down and my foot on the accelerator, our trip through Belldale with our hair flowing in the wind was fairly pleasant.

"You were right, he really doesn't like you," Pippa said. "He DEFINITELY still holds a grudge." Pippa mused over this for a second. "Do you think he could have killed Pierre to get back at you? Because you got through and he didn't?"

I sighed a little, pulling my sunglasses on. "He said he didn't even know I was there. And he seemed pretty convinced that HE was the one who got through."

"And do you believe him?"

I thought about that for a moment. "I'm not sure."

Chapter 6

"Pleaasssseee," Pippa begged, stretching out every vowel so that it sounded like the word had five syllables. She clasped her hands together. "I promise that he won't let you down."

My face was frozen in a look of shock and horror like I had been covered in lava at Pompeii and made to stand that way for all time.

Pippa waved her hand in front of my face. "Rach? Are you still alive in there?"

I was finally able to move my face. "Pippa, tell me this is one of your little jokes. You are pranking me, right?"

"I'm not, Rach! Marcello needs a job. Like, really needs one. I promise you he will be a model employee."

"Pippa, he breaks everything. He thinks that you can fish the glass out of salsa and still serve it! He drops hair everywhere!"

"I know he's not perfect..." Understatement. "But he can be trained. He'll be different at work than he is at home. You'll be there to keep an eye on him. And if he does totally mess up, you can fire him, and I promise there will be no hard feelings." Pippa grabbed me by the arms. "Please, just give him a chance, Rachael."

I couldn't believe I was about to agree to this. "Fine," I said with a heavy sigh. "I'll give him a chance. But this is on a trial basis only, okay?"

Pippa nodded and jumped up and down. I had to double check she understood what I mean. "Trial. Basis."

"Yes, Rach! Thank you!" She ran out of the kitchen and came back with Marcello, who was grinning ear to ear. He reached out for my hand and kissed it. "Thank you so much, Miss Rachael. I promise that I will be your humble servant at work. You will not regret this decision."

I was already regretting it, though. And I knew I would only regret it more when the next day came.

***

I hadn't taken my eyes off him from the moment he'd walked in the store.

"You know, you can trust him a little," Pippa whispered to me as she tied her apron behind her back. "It's not like he's going to burn the place down."

"Pippa, if he works here, it's on my terms. And that means never taking my eyes off him for one moment."

Pippa held her hands up. "Okay, okay, you got it, boss. Now, what do you want Marcello to do first?"

Hmm. Definitely nothing involving food, which was difficult in a bakery. Drinks maybe? I wondered just how badly he could screw up a cup of coffee.

"Does he know how to use a cappuccino machine?"

"I'm sure he can learn. He is Italian, after all!"

But as soon as the milk hit the frother and Marcello had managed to cover himself, me, and Pippa in hot milk before dropping the entire jug on the ground, I knew that he couldn't learn. At least, not until we were closed to customers and I had the time to teach him. And I'd had a few glasses of wine first.

"I'll get a mop."

While Marcello was in the cleaning closet—I figured there was only so much trouble he could get up to in there—I took a minute to check my phone.

I had a new message from Justin. **What happened yesterday with Renee and Adam???**

I'd been putting off messaging him. I wasn't yet sure what to make of either of them, they both could have done it, and I wanted to dig for some more information on both without Justin's opinions of them clouding my own good judgment.

I decided not to reply. Just as I was about to put my phone back in my pocket, a call from a private number flashed up on the screen.

I hovered over the 'reject' option before finally tapping it. I never answer calls from private numbers as a matter of principle. If it's someone I know, or it it's important, they can leave a message.

They did, but unfortunately not a text message. A voice message. I sighed and glanced towards the mop cupboard, wondering what was taking Marcello so long. *I really should go check on him.*

But with everything that was going on, I was worried the message could be important. Maybe it was Jackson. Maybe something had been discovered about Pierre.

I listened to the message while keeping one eye out for Marcello at the back of the shop.

"Hello...Rachael?" It was the kindly voice of an older woman, one that I thought I recognized but couldn't quite place. "I'm not sure this is the right number, I received it from Justin. Anyway," the voice continued briskly, if a little unsurely. "This is Dawn Ashfield calling, from *Baking Warriors*. I'm still in town. Production is in a bit of limbo right now, as you can imagine. But we have some good news for you. Give me a call back when you have a chance, dear," she said, before leaving her number.

Dawn Ashfield just called me? Well. Now I wished I had broken my stance on picking up calls from private numbers. I was just about to punch her number back in when I heard a squealing noise coming from the direction of the kitchen.

Or maybe the mop closet.

"What is that smell?" I muttered. Then I saw it. Gray smoke rising from the top of the door of the kitchen.

Pippa burst through the swinging doors coughing and spluttering. "Rach! Quick! Call the fire department!"

I sighed and began pressing the numbers. I didn't even have to ask how it had happened.

I wan't even surprised.

***

"To be fair to Marcello," Pippa said. "He didn't know that you weren't supposed to mix those two kinds of cleaning fluids...next to an open flame."

I surveyed the damage to the kitchen while we both hunched in together on the bottom part of a bench. Luckily a lot of it was superficial. And luckily we had more than one oven because one of them was doused in fire extinguishing foam.

I was more concerned with the loss of profits from the entire morning we'd had to close the shop.

"I'm sorry. I never should have asked if he could work here. But even I never thought he'd do this," she said, throwing her hands up at the blackened room.

"I thought he would do it," I said flatly. I wasn't even mad. I had been expecting something like this to happen. My only surprise was that it wasn't even worse.

"So I suppose he is fired then?"

I turned slowly towards Pippa. "Yes, Pippa. I think it's safe to say that the trial period was not a success."

Pippa sighed and stood up. "I'll help you clean up then. We can't stay shut all day."

"Umm," I muttered, distracted by my phone ringing again. I'd totally forgotten all about the phone call from Dawn. I still didn't know what this important news was she had to tell me. I glanced at Pippa, who started to scrub down a stovetop.

"Hey, you know what? You should go home and make sure Marcello is okay."

Pippa turned around in surprise. "Really?"

"Yeah, it's fine. I think we should just close for the day."

"Only if you're sure."

I was sure. Sure that I wanted to call Dawn Ashfield back and find out what the heck was going on. I was sure that if Dawn was calling me herself that the news must be important.

That meant I must be important.

Maybe filming is going ahead in secret. You know, they'd have to be a bit sensitive about it following Pierre's death...and I've been cast...and they just need to know when I'm available and how discreet I can be.

73

Man, I was starting to sound like Justin. Or Adam. It's just that the reality TV bug had bitten me hard. I needed to know what was happening with the show.

Pippa took her apron off. "So are you coming home with me?"

"Er, no. Are you all right to walk?" I asked her. "It's a bit cooler today so you should be fine. I've got some banking I need to take care of."

"Banking? Come on, Rachael, that's your go-to lie."

"It's not a lie this time. Promise."

As soon as Pippa was out the door, I punched Dawn's number into my phone.

"Hello, dear," she said, like she was a little surprised I'd actually called back. "I hope you're coping okay after everything that's happened."

"I'm sorry for your loss," I said. "I know that you and Pierre were very close."

"It's a tough time," she said. "Listen, Rachael, I've got something very important to tell you."

"Is it about the show?" I asked, a little too eagerly.

"It is," she replied. "Are you available to meet up sometime?"

"Yes, of course I am!" Way too eager again. "I am free right now actually."

She chuckled a little. "Right now might be a little too soon for me, dear. How about tomorrow?"

"Oh," I said, trying not to sound disappointed. "Yes, tomorrow is fine." I supposed there wasn't much point to closing down the bakery for the day now.

"Meet me down at the studio at 11:00 AM. I'll see you tomorrow."

***

"What should I wear?" I called out, running into the living room with a dress in each hand, only to come face to face with Pippa and Marcello engaging in a giant make-out session.

"Oh," I said, braking on my heels. "Sorry. I'll give you some space."

"No, Rach! It's fine," Pippa said, waving me back. "After all, this is your apartment."

Marcello was looking red-faced and sheepish. "Hello, Rachael." He straightened up, though Pippa was still half-draped over him. "I just want to assure you that I will pay you back for all the damage at the bakery. Just as soon as I get another job."

I tried not to open my eyes too wide at the mention of Marcello finding *another* job. Who would be crazy enough to hire him? I had to wonder what kind of job Marcello would even be suited for. Some place where he didn't have to make anything, touch anything, or take on any responsibilities. My mind was coming up blank.

"It's okay, Marcello. I've got insurance." But I had to wonder if insurance would cover an employee who wasn't even officially employed yet. I hadn't put Marcello on the books for his 'trial' period. Anyway, I had bigger things to worry about. Like what to wear for my meeting with Dawn Ashfield in the morning.

"Does it even matter?" Pippa asked. Pippa was the kind of girl who could be 'girly' in certain ways—take marrying a perfect stranger and gushing about his every eccentricity like a love sick puppy, for instance—but who was completely ungirly at other times. Take clothes, for instance. She wasn't the kind of girl to gush over outfits. She didn't even like shopping. So I wasn't surprised when I held up the dresses to ask "Blue or purple?" and her eyes glazed over.

"It *does* matter. I need to impress Dawn. Pippa, I think this is a sort of secret audition. Or maybe we're even going to start filming. After all, Justin told me I was practically a shoe-in to make the cut. And Dawn has influence on the show, you know. Without Pierre around, she probably makes the final decision. I'm kinda nervous."

"Well, I think either dress is fine." Pippa frowned. "But don't get your hopes up too high. She could want to see you about anything."

Just then my phone started to ring. "That's probably... Oh! It's Justin." At first I was a little disappointed, but then I realized something. "Pips, if Justin is calling me then that DEFINITELY means that filming is back on!"

Pippa went back to kissing Marcello while I took the phone call. "Justin?" I said excitedly. "I think I know what this phone call is about."

"You do?" he asked, cutting me off.

"Yes," I said, holding up the blue dress in front of the full-length mirror in the hall. "It's about the show, right?" I lowered my voice in a cheeky, conspiratorial manner. "It's about filming, isn't it?"

"Yes, it is," Justin said, surprised. "Oh, so you already know that filming is being put on hold indefinitely."

I dropped the dress. "Excuse me?"

"I'm having to call all the auditionees," Justin said with a sigh, showing just how over it all he was. "Tell them all that the show is technically 'on hiatus' until this whole Pierre business is sorted out. Basically, if the show ever comes back--and I mean IF--then we'll have to hold all the auditions again."

I was stunned into silence. "But, Justin, I thought you said Pierre liked me, that I was going through to the next round."

"Pierre did like you," Justin said, just a little too pointedly, I thought. "But Pierre is dead, Rachael. He won't have much sway over who gets on the show from beyond the grave."

I moved into my bedroom and slumped down on my bed. "I just thought... Never mind."

Justin must have heard my glumness. "Hey, it's okay. You can audition again. You were great."

"So you said."

Justin clucked his tongue and lowered his voice. "I don't suppose you had a chance to speak to Adam and Renee, did you?"

"I did, actually. Still forming my conclusions there."

"Ha." I could hear Justin's heavy sigh down the end of the line. "Honey, I just got off the phone with Adam myself, and let me tell you, he is ECSTATIC over the news."

"Ecstatic? Why is that?"

"Well, honey, he knew he didn't get through. He blew his audition, and not just in the 'kind of' blew it way that you did. I mean, his cake was *inedible*. Maybe we could have pushed him through if he had any kind of personality to speak of on the day, but he totally froze up, and not even in an entertaining way. Pierre hated him. We'd already sent him home that day WELL before Pierre's body was found."

Hang on. But Adam said he'd heard the screams when Pierre had been found.

And that wasn't the only thing he'd told me.

"But Adam told me that he'd gone through to the next round. Or at least that he was pretty sure he had."

"Nope," Justin replied. "We'd told him thanks but no thanks. Try again next year. So, you can imagine that this is all very good news to him. If we rehold auditions then Adam gets another shot." Justin sighed. "Not that I think he has what it takes, but hey, I'm just the genius producer of the whole thing. Rachael? Are you still there?"

"Er, yes," I said, standing up. I'd been lost in my own thoughts. "I have to go, Justin. Thanks for calling."

"Hey, Rachael," he whispered again. "You ARE still working on trying to clear my name, right?"

"I am Justin. That's why I've got to go. I think I better make another visit to Adam Ali."

Chapter 7

"Dawn?" I asked tentatively, as I stuck my neck into the greenroom like a nervous gander. No one there.

Hmm.

Maybe I should just leave. After all, there was no way that Dawn wanted to confide in me about my top secret casting on *Baking Warriors*. I cringed now, remembering that I'd been so sure of her intentions, so sure that I'd made it on TV. What made me cringe even harder was how much I'd wanted it to be true.

My heart started to thud a little. *What if it's bad news she wants to tell me?* Maybe she wanted to tell me that my audition was so abhorrent that I should never bother embarrassing myself by trying again.

I should just leave. I need to talk to Adam.

"Hello, dear!"

I stifled a scream as I managed to control myself from jumping out of my skin. Dawn was standing behind me with a big, warm grin on her face that immediately put me at ease. She was probably only old enough to be my mother, but she had that 'grandmotherly' vibe about her that made you want to spend the afternoon with her baking cookies. Or just being taken care of by her.

For a few seconds I missed my own grandmother. I was ashamed to find that I could feel tears beginning to prick my eyes and I quickly turned away.

"Oh, heavens, are you okay, dear?" Dawn placed a hand on my arm and stroked it gently. That, unfortunately, only made the tears fiercer.

"I'm fine," I said quickly, putting a bright smile on my face. "Just had a silly moment there."

Dawn smiled sympathetically. "I suppose you've heard that filming has been delayed indefinitely. But don't worry, dear, you'll be able to audition again when the time comes. I'm sure you'll be on the top of the producer's lists. Is that what's got you so upset?"

I shook my head quickly. "No. Geesh, I hope I wouldn't cry just because a TV show was being delayed. I hope I'm not quite that desperate to be famous." Was I though? I wondered if the disappointment of the news Justin had given me was actually mixing together with my sudden grief and making me feel more emotional than I would have otherwise.

I didn't want Dawn to think me that shallow. "I'm just missing my grandma today." I glanced around the studio where the *Baking Warriors* logos and branding still stood, all pink and white lettering with puffs of flour and sugar surrounding the font. "She was the one who taught me to bake." I bowed my head. "I thought that being on the show might make her proud. Well, if she can still be proud of me, wherever she is now." I took a deep breath. "She passed away a few years ago, just before I opened my bakery. She never got to see that either."

"Oh, I'm sorry, dear. Come on, why don't we go grab a coffee and we can talk about it." She smiled that warm smile at me and I teared up again, but nodded, grateful for the opportunity.

The venue Dawn had chosen didn't exactly thrill me.

But as we walked through the automatic doors of Bakermatic, I smiled anyway and offered a polite nod to the manager, Simona, as I slid into the booth across from Dawn.

"I love this place," Dawn said, glancing around the store. "So bright and yellow. Like happiness."

The place hadn't exactly caused me a great deal of happiness. For a while there, the low prices and underhanded practices of Bakermatic had threatened to put my boutique bakery out of business. But we had reached a sort of truce these days. Meaning, basically, that we just stayed out of each other hair, and Simona didn't send staff down the road to hand out fliers in the front of my store.

"I'll order," I said. "What would you like?"

Dawn said she'd have a cappuccino and a brownie. I had to bite my tongue to stop from pointing out that none of the cakes were baked on the premises and that they arrived in plastic, filled with preservatives. Whatever Dawn Ashfield wanted, Dawn Ashfield got, as far as I was concerned.

It was a little awkward when I finally got to the counter to order from Simona, but not for the reason I'd originally thought it would be.

Simona wasn't quite looking at me as I ordered the cappuccino, brownie, and a vanilla latte for myself. I thought we were over the whole mortal enemies thing so I was a little surprised.

"How's business been?" I asked, as casually and as friendly as I could.

Simona just nodded as she punched the orders into a tablet screen. "Sugar?" she asked as her long black ponytail swung forward, covering her face and almost obscuring her words.

"Er..." I hadn't asked Dawn. "Just a couple of packets on the side."

Simona finally looked at me. Then her gaze drifted out the window to where the tents filled with press still stood to form a makeshift campsite. "So, is what they are saying true, Rachael?"

I shrugged, unsure. "That depends on what they are saying." I thought about Justin still holed up in his hotel room. "I know they are trying to pin it on one of the producers, but I was there and I don't think he did it." I wasn't really sure I ought to be speculating like that. I also wasn't sure why I was in such a rush to trip over myself to defend Justin.

Simona made a face as though she had no idea what I was talking about. "No," she said, lowering her voice into a whisper. "I'm talking about the rumors about you and Pierre."

I felt my face redden. The creep of the blush must have been slow at first but after a few seconds, my cheeks burned like a furnace and I was certain I must be red as a tomato. "That's...that's in the press?" I whispered. I glanced over my shoulder in dismay to look at Dawn.

Did she know?

Oh, this was so humiliating.

"I'm sorry, Rachael. I assumed you knew."

I shook my head. "I haven't looked at any of the news," I mumbled, grabbing my sugar packets and taking them back to the table. I'd been avoiding all the press coverage so that it didn't influence my investigation. Now their glowering glares and sniggers the other morning made so much more sense.

I slunk into the plastic booth, wishing that the yellow seat would swallow me up.

"You okay, dear?"

Simona delivered the coffees to the table and I muttered another thanks. My hand was trembling as I ripped the sugar packet open and dumped the contents into my latte.

I had to ask. "Dawn," I started to whisper, before we were approached by a young woman in her early twenties with a short mahogany colored bob and a purple pea coat.

"Sorry," she said, her voice gushing. "But, you're Dawn Ashfield, aren't you?"

I paused, stirring my coffee and looking at Dawn, waiting anxiously for her response. Would she be annoyed at being interrupted like this?

It was clear this sort of thing must happen to her all the time. She graciously posed for a photo while the girl, practically bouncing up and down with excitement, aimed her smart phone at the two of them, her arm around Dawn. "Thank you so much!" she squealed, before running off.

"I suppose you get that quite a lot," I said, taking a sip of my latte before scanning the room. I hadn't noticed it when we'd first walked in, but now I saw that half the people in the shop were casting furtive glances in Dawn's direction and whispering to each other to check amongst themselves if it was really her, wondering if they had the nerve to come over and ask for a photo like that one brave girl had.

Dawn waved her hand and picked up her cappuccino. "Oh, it's all just part of the job. I've been at this a long time, dear. It's become second nature over the decades. I've come to expect the constant interruptions. Water off a duck's back now."

I nodded but I was trying not to frown. I knew that Dawn had been baking for a long time. She was one of those faces that occasionally turned up on morning TV shows when I was little. She had also published dozens of cookbooks over the years, but it wasn't until she'd been cast as a judge on *Baking Warriors* five years earlier that she'd actually gotten truly famous.

Anyway. I supposed she knew better than I did when it came to her own experience.

"You were asking me something, right before that young lady came over?"

I was suddenly too embarrassed to ask if Dawn knew anything about the rumors about me and Pierre. I was sure that if she did know about them—and surely she did—then she would be discreet about it.

I cleared my throat. "I was just wondering, Dawn. Not that I'm not thrilled to be having coffee with you, but why did you want to meet up with me? Does it have something to do with the show?"

Dawn chuckled a little. "You are anxious to be on the show, aren't you, dear?" She reached over and placed a hand on mine and it felt warm and leathery. "But take if from me, dear, fame isn't all it's cracked up to be." She took a sip of coffee and ended with a heavy sigh. "Take it from Pierre."

"Right." She still hadn't answered my question though. "I'm sorry about Pierre, by the way. I know the two of you were close friends." They were always in magazine features together, raving about how they couldn't live without the friendship and support of the other while they were filming. "It must be tough for you right now."

Dawn stared down into her coffee cup. "Yes," she whispered. "To be honest, though, it still hasn't quite hit me. Maybe once we're all out of this town. Nothing really feels real at the moment while we are all in limbo." She lifted her eyes and I caught sight of tears sitting in the bottom of them. "By the way, dear, I don't believe any of those salacious rumors about you and Pierre. I was there. I know you only met him the one time. But, you know, people do talk."

I could feel my face redden.

"Don't worry, sweetheart. They've gotta have something to fill the magazines and websites with. It's only because you did so well at the audition. People were jealous, I guess." She settled back in her seat. "If Pierre hadn't been killed, then you likely would have been the one to go through to the next round. And you didn't even use that sad backstory about your grandma!" She must have caught sight of my face because she looked immediately stricken and hurried to apologize. "You must forgive me. Years of working in reality TV have rubbed off on me. I'm starting to sound like a producer. All this talk about backstory, like the events aren't real things that have traumatized people. Please, you must tell me a little about your grandmother."

I nodded and told her about how she started to teach me how to bake when I was just three years old. "My mother had me when she was very young. She was single and had to work full time to support me, so we moved back in with my grandma. Nana was the person who looked after me full time from when I was just a few months old, right up until I started school." I recounted some of my best memories to Dawn, of the way Nana had taught me about the science of baking, as she called it. She baked every thing with precise measurements, always used a pair of finely tuned scales to make sure there was the exact right amount of flour, sugar, butter, etc., in a dish, never ever eyeballed it, and knew that you couldn't just double the ingredients in a recipe and expect it to taste the same. "Recipes are there for a reason," she would always say.

"Even though it could occasionally be frustrating, I learned a lot from her strictness, and everything she taught me has stuck with me." I grew quiet for a moment. "She passed away only a few months before the store opened. I always wish I'd brought the date forward, but I was my grandma's granddaughter. I waited until everything was perfect before I went forward."

"You must really miss her," Dawn said gently.

"I do."

"I hope all this death business hasn't gone and stirred all that up." Dawn paused. "But I guess you're used to grisly murders now, aren't you?" She shivered a little. "The kind of thing I avoid. I can't even watch a scary movie or read a crime novel. What has drawn you to try and solve these cases, dear? It's a rather peculiar hobby, if you ask me."

I was a teeny bit taken aback. "I wouldn't say I've ever gone looking for these things, or pursued them. They just seem to find me. Wherever there's a murder, there I am." I made a face, though I tried to cover it up with a little laugh. "That's probably more morbid than if I had gone looking for them, isn't it?"

Dawn shrugged a little. "For some people, tragedy just seems to follow them."

I wasn't sure that was it. I had no idea why these sorts of things seemed to follow me around. "I do know that I seem to have a knack for solving these cases, though."

Dawn's eyebrow shot up a little. "Don't tell me your investigating Pierre's death?"

I wasn't quite sure how candid I should be. After all, it was all on a very hush-hush basis. Unofficial, as Jackson would say. "I wouldn't say investigating. I'm just keeping my eyes and ears open."

Dawn looked impressed. "Well, I hope you do manage to turn something up. The sooner we are out of this town and away from the press scrutiny the better. I'm as desperate as anyone to know what happened to Pierre and I can't say I've got all that much faith in your local police department. Please tell me you will look into it, Rachael."

I wondered how Jackson would feel to know that it wasn't just the locals who had lost confidence in the Belldale police department. Even the out-of-towners were skeptical.

"I can't promise anything, Dawn. But I will try my best." I placed my empty latte glass down. "You never told me why you wanted to meet with me."

Dawn rested her face in her hands and gave me a warm smile. "I just wanted to check in with you, Rachael. Have a coffee. Chat. And we've done that." She grabbed her purse and extended her smile even wider. "You remind me an awful lot of myself when I was your age. And I wanted to offer to mentor you at any time. If you're interested, that is."

My eyes grew wide. "Interested? I'm more than interested. Dawn, I'm sort of taken aback right now. Are you really willing to do that?"

She chuckled again. "Of course, my dear. But right now, I really need to be getting back to my hotel. Justin wants to see me for something, and you know how persuasive he is!"

I followed her out of the shop. "Oh, I know it."

***

The apartment looked like a bomb had gone off. For a second I had to wonder if that was what had actually happened. It wasn't just a matter of mess—though as I stepped over the piles of clothes and books on the floor, I almost tripped and sprained my ankle—but there was also debris lying on the floor. Broken bits of wood, some glass, trinkets lying everywhere.

"Did we have an earthquake?" I asked as Pippa appeared in the hallway. Maybe I'd been so wrapped up in my meeting with Dawn that I hadn't even felt it. Maybe it had been confined to our apartment.

"Sorry, Rach," Pippa said, making an awkward face. "We weren't expecting you back so soon." She spun around and looked at an overturned bookshelf that no longer had any shelves in tact. That explained the debris all over the floor. "Marcello was moving some of his bags and he wasn't watching where he was going."

There was a surprise. "Did he also have a bull trailing behind him?" I asked in disbelief before following her into the living room. "Hang on," I said, staring at the piles of bags and luggage. "He was moving bags INTO the house?"

"Yes?" Pippa said unsurely. "I know they are taking up a bit of space."

"Pippa, I assumed he'd be moving his bags OUT of here, by now."

Pippa's face fell. "You don't want us here anymore?"

I sighed. "It's not that I don't want you here. You know I always said you could live here as long as you want or need, Pippa. But that was when you were single. This is a one-bedroom apartment! We can't have three people living here! Especially when one of them is..." I bit my tongue to keep from saying something I would later regret. "...Marcello."

"I see," Pippa said, crossing her arms and refusing to look at me. "You don't like Marcello. Well, don't worry, Rachael. We will be out of your hair as soon as we can! We won't put you out any longer. "

"It's not like that, Pippa. And it's not that I don't like Marcello as a person," I said, exasperated. It was true. I did like him. It was just that... "I just like not having my stuff ruined every day."

Pippa's face dropped and her indignation drained away a little. "I know he can be a hassle to live with," she said quietly. "Honestly, I appreciate you putting up with us as long as you have." She caught sight of the mess in the hallway. "I'll help you clean that up."

"Don't worry just now," I said, grabbing her arm. "It can wait 'til later. Let's just have a quiet night in. Eat some snacks, watch some Criminal Point. Marcello is at his new job washing dishes tonight, right?" Pippa nodded. "So, what do you say?"

"I say, sounds great," Pippa said with a forced smile, before wrapping her arms around my neck. "Thanks, Rach. And I promise, we'll find our own place as soon as possible. If not sooner."

***

"So, stop keeping me in suspense. What did Dawn have to say for herself? Are you getting cast on *Baking Warriors* or not?" Pippa sat back on the sofa, curling her knees up underneath her with wide eyes, waiting for my answer.

I stuck my chopsticks in the carton of gluten-free satay rice noodles and shook my head as I stared up at her from my position on the floor. "You were right, I shouldn't have gotten my hopes up. Filming is delayed indefinitely. I will have to re-audition if I ever want a chance of getting on the show." I took another mouthful of noodles. "I'm not even sure I still want to, to be honest."

Pippa leaned forward. "But, Rach, you've got to," she whispered. "Otherwise, whoever killed Pierre is going to get just what they wanted. You can't let them actually receive their bizarre sense of justice."

I shrugged. "Or, I could just find the person who did it."

Pippa shrugged as well. "I guess. I still want to see you on TV though. You've got to do it for me if you won't do it for yourself." She munched down on her own cashew and vegetable stir fry noodles. "So what were you summoned to the studio for then?"

"Huh? Oh. Dawn Ashfield just wanted to talk to me to see if I wanted her to mentor me. It was kind of a surprise."

Pippa raised an eyebrow, impressed. "See! Now you've GOT to re-audition. It would be crazy not to. You could do worse than Dawn Ashfield for a mentor. Cripes, you'll probably win the whole thing if Dawn takes you under her wing."

"That's the truth." I dug around for some more noodles before stuffing them into my mouth. "I guess I'll have to think about it, weigh all the options." I thought about my nana again for a second.

"That's not a wedding cake," she replied.

"Well, it's white."

"That's because it's white chocolate," Pippa said quickly. "Other cakes besides wedding cakes can be white, you know."

Adam narrowed his eyes and bowed down to get a better look at the cake. "That looks like fondant to me," he said.

"It's not. It's white chocolate. Regular old icing. It's just extra smooth. We have a special spatula that we use." Pippa looked over at me for help.

"Adam," I said, and he finally turned his attention to me. "Can we help you with anything this morning?" I was thinking that he could certainly help us with something, but I didn't want to make him any crosser than he already was before I started to interrogate him.

He finally managed to pry his nose away from the display stand. He pointed to Pippa before saying, "I was trying to track down this one. To see if she had any actual intention of purchasing one of my prestigious wedding cakes. But now I can see she has no intention to. Why would she buy from me when the shop she works in supplies wedding cakes?" He finished pointedly, glaring at me with his icy blue eyes.

Seeing as he was already irritated and had no plans of backing down or playing nice, I decided I may as well come right out and ask him.

"Why did you lie about knowing I was at the audition?"

With his red hair and pale skin, it didn't take much of a blush for Adam to turn bright red. "I didn't lie," he said feebly, reaching out to tap his fingers on one of my counter tops. "I had no idea you were there, darling. Why would you say otherwise?"

I straightened up and exchanged a look with Pippa. "Justin told me. He told me that not only did you know I was there, you knew that I did better than you. That I was going through and you weren't." I hesitated, wondering if I ought to really stick the boot in. "Justin told me that you bombed your audition, actually."

Adam performed the motion of flicking his hair over his shoulder even though his hair was nowhere near long enough to actually do that.

"Justin doesn't know what he is talking about," Adam mumbled, not taking his eyes away from the cake display. I thought I could detect a note of bitterness in his voice that wasn't there due to any shame or embarrassment over screwing up his audition. I exchanged a look with Pippa, who seemed to pounce on the tone in his voice.

"Did you get along with Justin while you were preparing to interview?"

Adam lifted his head high in the air and pouted. "As well as anyone could get along with that guy. With his ridiculous expectations and his air of self importance."

Pippa and I were still looking at each other. Whatever Adam's problem was with Justin, it was personal, not professional.

I cleared my throat and ventured a guess. "Adam, did you perhaps get along a little too well with Justin?"

Adam was still pouting but he threw me an indignant look. "Whatever it was that happened between us, it was all one way, let me tell you. I turned Justin down and he responded by blowing my audition for me."

"Adam, I'm sure Justin wouldn't do that."

"He did. He tampered with my audition piece. I just know it. Left the cake out of the fridge or something so it tasted bad. I've never seen a person spit out one of my creations in my life, and suddenly all the judges are spitting my cake out, saying it was one of the worst things they have ever tasted." Adam shook his head. "No. It was Justin screwing with it. It just had to have been. I'm telling you, he wanted to take revenge on me for rejecting him. That was it." Adam finally looked me directly in the eyes. "Well, now I will have my chance again. A total do-over. With any luck, Justin won't be working at the show by the time the new auditions roll around."

"Adam," I said slowly. Accusingly. "Why you think that Justin won't be around? What did you do?"

He didn't answer me.

"Are you the one that leaked the rumors to the press that Justin was the one who did it?"

Adam's attention was fixed back firmly on the cake display. "Maybe."

"Adam!"

"Well, I had to get revenge on him somehow! He ruined my one big chance to make it."

I threw my head back in frustration. I had Justin holed up in a hotel room, constantly texting me asking whether I had found the killer yet so that he was off the hook, and the entire rumor was down to a lover's spat.

Adam kept trying to defend himself. "If Justin is kicked off the show then I will get a fair chance. It's only fair. He deserves it if he's going to tamper with the outcome of the show!"

I rolled me eyes a little. "That's a producer's job, Adam. To tamper with the outcome of a show." I stopped and stared at him.

I had to ask it.

But Pippa jumped in ahead of me.

"So it looks like Pierre's murder worked out pretty well for you," Pippa started to say slowly, inching her way towards a squirming Adam.

"Well, maybe, but only accidentally." Adam straightened up and cleared his throat. "What are you trying to suggest?"

"Did you kill Pierre so that you could take revenge on Justin? Or Pierre, for that matter. For spitting your cake out."

"No!" Adam squealed. "I might have been angry about losing my chance, but I would never do something like that. That's insane."

He held his hand up to his neck to mimic a pearl-clutching motion. Pippa and I looked at each other. I knew we were both thinking the same thing. *How can we trust a word this guy is saying?*

Adam looked at me. "Anyway, I'm not the only person making up rumors and selling them to the press," he said pointedly.

"What are you talking about, Adam?"

He raised an eyebrow. "Don't you want to know how the rumor about you and Pierre got leaked to the press?"

I sighed. I did want to know, but I didn't really want to give Adam the satisfaction that he was clearly deriving from being the holder of this information.

Pippa nodded at me. A signal to me to drop my pride.

"Fine, Adam. Tell me who told the press about that."

He shrugged. "I don't know her too well. Just met her at the audition. Some single mother with five kids. When you got through ahead of her, she kind of lost it. Said she was sure that you must have used more than just your baking skills to impress Pierre. And when Pierre died, she told me she was going straight to the press." He shrugged. "Said she thought it would make you look guilty."

Chapter 8

"Are you ready?" Pippa asked me as I took a deep breath.

"Yes. It's time I finally faced up to this."

Pippa stepped back and looked over my shoulder as I finally brought up the news headlines that had been running constantly since Pierre's death.

"And I've got an actual real life paper here for you as well, if you need it," Pippa said.

I could feel the waft of air on the back of my neck as she waved the newspaper behind me. "That's super helpful."

"Ohhh." I could hear Pippa whispering behind me. I could hear the wince in her voice. "It's pretty bad."

The gossip sites were plastered with garish photos of Pierre and me, badly photoshopped into them with headlines like "*Baking Warriors* Love Scandal - Contestant Cheats Her Way In."

"This is insane, Pippa. We never even had a photo taken together. We never even met except for that one time at my disastrous audition."

When Pippa didn't say anything, I swung around in my chair to find her making a confused face that she quickly tried to straighten before I saw it. "What?"

"Well, I thought you said your audition went really well. Isn't that why you were going through to the next round?"

"Well," I said, a little unsure. "I *thought* my audition went badly. Pierre didn't seem to like my cake, but Justin assured me that he did really like me."

"Oh."

"Pippa! It's not like that!"

She glanced over my shoulder back at the gossip sites. "No, I'm sure it's not."

"It's not, Pippa!" But I had to cross my arms over my chest as I thought about it all. "Justin just said that Pierre had to pretend not to like my cake for TV. It's all fake, you know. Just like these news stories," I said pointedly.

Pippa nodded firmly. "I know. Sorry, Rach. It's just that they can be pretty convincing."

I spun back around to face the computer. "Yeah, well, Renee did a pretty good job of spinning a good tale for them. She's mixed enough true details from the audition process in with the lies so that it seems more convincing." I dropped my face into my hands.

This was all so embarrassing. I was only glad that my nana wasn't around to see my public humiliation. Even the thought of her reading these gossip articles made me want the earth to swallow me.

"So, what are you thinking?" Pippa asked. She settled down, perched up on the desk next to me.

"If Renee killed Pierre, it makes sense that she would try to frame someone else as a suspect. It's a pretty good plan. Maybe not the most original, but a solid plan nonetheless."

Pippa clucked her tongue a few times, in deep concentration. "To be fair, though, or maybe her plan just backfired, but people don't really seem to be blaming you for his death if you actually read the articles. They are more focused on the scandal of it. Of the fact that you cheated your way through."

"Hmm," I murmured. She was right. Not that I'd cheated my way through, but that no one was really pointing the finger at me. They thought I had a crush on Pierre, not that I was trying to kill him. "Either way though, it takes the attention off the actual crime. That could have been a smart move on her part. She was desperate to get on the show, Pippa. Just like Adam was. She might have been just as upset as Adam was when she missed out. Pierre's death benefits her as much as it did Adam."

I slumped back on the sofa. "Just about the only person his death doesn't benefit is me."

"Exactly. Maybe Renee didn't fully think that angle though before she leaked the story to the press. Her plan failed."

I sat up. "But why would she even do it in the first place? Was she really that angry at me for making it to the next round over her? Unless she did kill Pierre, I can't see why she would do such a thing."

Pippa checked the time. "It's late. Almost 9:00. Do you think we should go over there tonight?"

"She has young children, Pippa. They might be sleeping. Besides, if she was really a dangerous menace to society, surely the Belldale Police would be on to her by now."

We each looked at each other before we burst out laughing. "Well, maybe not." Pippa reached over for her tea and took a big slurp. "Speaking of the police, have you heard from Jackson lately?"

I shook my head and pursed my lips. "Nope. Ever since I turned him down—I mean as an investigator, Pippa, don't let your imagination run wild—he seems to be avoiding me."

"Sulking?"

I sighed. "I don't know. I can't presume to know what goes on in his head."

"And he's still living with that skinny detective, right?"

"As far as I know." I was eager to change the subject. "Speaking of living with partners. Have you and Marcello had any luck finding a place to live yet?" I asked hopefully.

"Ooh!" Pippa jumped up and pushed me off the seat so that she could get to the computer. She quickly brought up a real estate site and excitedly showed me the listing for a two-bedroom apartment at a rock bottom price.

I leaned forward. "That's half what I pay and it's double the space."

"Yep." Pippa nodded as she flicked through the photos. "There's a proper bath as well. And there's a big yard, if we want to get a dog. The landlord allows pets, apparently."

"Pippa, what's the catch?" I suddenly caught the address of the property. "Pippa, this is over the other side of the highway! It's in downtown Belldale," I said, really trying to hide the look of horror on my face. I don't like to be a snob, but Belldale is definitely a town of two halves. I'd only been to this area once before in my life, when Pippa had dragged me to a meeting of her paranormal club.

"I know," she said cheerfully. "The area is about to blow up big time."

"It is?"

She nodded. "So we should grab this place now before rent prices go up."

I sat in silence for a moment. There was another reason I wasn't that keen on Pippa's new zip code. Well, technically, that side of town shared the same zip code, but it may as well have been on a different continent as far as I was concerned. "But, Pippa, it's so far away."

"Don't worry," she replied. "I'll still make it to work on time every day."

"It's not that, Pips. It's that you won't be able to just pop over for a coffee or a chat whenever you want." I stared at the empty sofa. It suddenly hit me that Pippa wouldn't be living on my couch anymore.

It suddenly hit me that she was *married.*

And it didn't seem to be one of her crazy schemes, or something she got sick of and gave up on after a few weeks.

She really loved Marcello. She was serious about him.

And she was really going to move in with him.

"Rach? You okay?" Pippa said with concerned, leaning back to look at me.

"Yeah," I said quickly, trying to hide the sniffling sound in my voice. "It's just been kind of an emotional day for me, that's all."

I stood up. "Let me know if you need me for a reference," I said with a big smile. "For when you apply."

Pippa made an apologetic face. "We kind of already did apply. Fingers crossed, we'll hear by tomorrow."

"Oh." I sucked in a deep breath. "That's great, Pips," I said before I gave her a big hug. "I'll cross all my fingers. And toes as well."

***

I heard Pippa make a sort of inhuman cry that I couldn't tell if it was a squeal of joy or disappointment.

I ran into the front of the bakery from the kitchen, my hands still covered with flour and held up daintily with my elbows bent, as I ran over to Pippa, who ended the call on her cell phone.

"Well?" I asked, assuming it had been her real estate agent on the phone. In the split second before she answered, I wasn't sure whether I wanted her to get the apartment or not.

We can all squeeze in together. It hasn't been THAT chaotic. We can make it work!

Hang on. What about Marcello? It HAS been that chaotic. It's been very chaotic.

Pippa grinned at me. "You're going to be happy!"

Was I?

"We got the apartment!" She started jumping up and down and raced over to hug me. I joined her in jumping up and down but tried to keep my floury hands away from her. We must have looked a strange sight to the people walking past.

"I am happy," I said. "Happy for you. I have to admit, Pippa, that when I first met Marcello..."

"Yes?"

"Well, I wondered if you had really thought it through. You have to admit the marriage was a bit of a rush, and Marcello is a bit eccentric to live with."

"And now?" she asked expectantly.

"Well, now I think that Marcello is a complete and utter disaster. But, Pippa, he's your complete and utter disaster. And that's all that matters."

"Thanks, Rach."

"Well, I guess we may as well start packing when we get home." I accidentally clapped my hands together sending a puff of flour bursting into the air. "I'll help you, don't worry."

"We'll have three pairs of hands then," Pippa said.

"Won't Marcello be at his dishwashing job?"

She made a face. "He kind of already got fired from that. He broke twenty-five plates on his first night."

"Of course he did."

***

"Umm," I said cautiously, as I watched Marcello pick up a knife to slice through the packing tape. "I'm just a little concerned," I whispered to Pippa. "First, I thought we were putting stuff into boxes, not taking stuff out. Second, should Marcello really be holding a knife?"

"We need to open some of the boxes we've already packed. Marcello says he accidentally packed the keys for the new apartment and we can't find them anywhere."

"Right. And the other point I brought up?"

"He'll be fine, Rach. Marcello isn't a child. He's a fully-grown man. He can be trusted with a knife."

"Okay. You're right. Of course." I slowly turned my attention to the box I myself was packing. Marcello's bags had only arrived a few days earlier, but he'd somehow managed to unpack every last one of them so they all needed to be re-packed. Then there was Pippa's stuff. "I think we're going to be here all night," I murmured. "Especially if you want to move into the new apartment in the morning."

Suddenly I heard a scream followed by what I could only assume were expletives in Italian. I spun around to see blood spurting out of Marcello's hand as he lifted it up in the air.

"Oh, sweetheart!" Pippa said, racing over to him. "Oh my gosh, the knife has gone right through."

"Oh my," I exclaimed, taking a step back as my head began to grow foggy. I could feel it happening, could feel the strength draining from my legs. If I didn't sit down, I was going to faint.

I almost made it to the sofa before I collapsed. My legs were against the sofa while I was laying flat on my back.

"Rach!" I heard Pippa scream. She ran over to me and tapped me on the cheek.

I was groggy, but conscious. "I'm fine," I said, swatting her hand away. "Just give me a second. Go focus on Marcello."

She ran back over to a still-bleeding Marcello. "Here, use this shirt to stop the blood." I had my eyes open a peek and could just make out the image of Pippa wrapping a white shirt around Marcello's index finger.

"Oh shoot! This isn't my shirt! Sorry, Rachael!"

I closed my eyes again and waved my hand. That was the least of my worries right then. I reached up to my forehead and tried to take a few deep breaths. I didn't like being so hopeless while someone clearly needed my help.

I wobbled onto my feet and made my way over to where Marcello was hopelessly flailing about. "I think you should tie that shirt a little tighter around the wound."

Pippa turned to me.

"I'm so sorry, Rachael! I've got to get Marcello to the emergency room."

I waved my hand, still a little uneasy on my feet. "No, it's fine. Of course you do." I ushered them out of the room, Marcello clutching my white shirt around his finger. The blood slowly seeping into it was turning the whole thing various shades of red and pink like an extra bloody sunset.

I swallowed. *Just accept that it's a write off, Rachael. It's not worth getting upset over. At least it wasn't anything more serious. At least Marcello only stabbed himself.*

"I'll keep packing while you're gone," I assured them as I followed them out to the car.

"Rach, you don't have to do that."

"Trust me, if I know the Belldale Hospital Emergency Room, you won't be getting out of there for six or seven hours."

I caught Marcello wince. "Well, maybe five if you're really lucky," I tried unsuccessfully to reassure him.

I closed the driver's side door for Pippa and she sped off into the night.

"I guess it's just you and me now," I said to my glass of wine as I took several gulps, hoping it would calm my nerves a little after the sight of all that blood. I thought back to my earlier conversation with Dawn, thinking how funny it was that she thought I would purposely pursue crime solving when I would faint at the first sign of blood.

With my disposition returning to normal, I sighed a little as I looked around at all the carnage strewn across the floor. "How did he manage to make this much mess when his bags only arrived a few days ago?"

I stopped myself. I knew perfectly well how he had managed to do it. He was Marcello.

Trouble followed him.

I supposed I could relate to that, so maybe I should be a little more understanding of his trials and tribulations. Pippa sure seemed to have infinite patience for him. But they were newlyweds. What was going to happen when the sheen wore off and Pippa was stuck living with a walking disaster?

I opened a box and started filling it with the odds and ends that were littering the floor. Books, postcards, old notepads, and photos.

I was still a little shaky, so when I scooped up the first handful of books and photographs, they slid out onto the floor. I slumped down on the sofa and placed my head between my knees for a second.

Come on, Rachael. Pull it together. You've got a long night of packing ahead of you.

I lifted my head and forced myself to keep going. But as I scooped the pile up again, another photo slid out and fluttered to the floor before it landed face down. Once I'd stuffed the rest of the items into a box, I reached down and picked up the photo, turning it over absentmindedly, expecting, I suppose, to find a photo of

Marcello as a child in Italy or maybe a more recent photo, perhaps one taken at his and Pippa's shotgun wedding.

But that's not what I found.

Staring back at me was a smiling Marcello with his arm wrapped around Pierre Hamilton.

What the?

No. It can't be.

I turned the photo over again. As though the back of it might give me some clue as to whether it was real or not. To be honest, it had been some time since I'd held a real photo in my hands. But as far as I could tell, it wasn't doctored in any way.

How on earth did Marcello know Pierre Hamilton?

And why had he arrived in Belldale the day before Pierre was killed?

Suddenly the weariness returned to my legs, and this time it wasn't caused by the blood stains in the carpet.

Chapter 9

My head was still spinning the following morning when Marcello and Pippa finally returned home from the emergency room at 5:00 AM. Even when I closed my eyes, the dizziness remained, my bed becoming a life raft that I tried to cling onto. Trying to sleep was fruitless.

Pippa poked her head in my room to whisper that Marcello was all stitched up and ready to survive another day. "Well, maybe," she whispered.

I was lying with my back to her, facing the wall. I pretended to be asleep, trying not to breath or make a single movement.

"Well, goodnight then," Pippa said before tiptoeing away. She flicked the hall light off and I finally breathed a little.

This was not how I wanted our last night living together to go. And I wasn't just talking about Marcello's accident.

I didn't want to be lying in the dark, wondering if I was living with a killer. Wondering if it was even safe to close my eyes.

But how could I possibly bring this up with Pippa? She was smitten with the guy. She'd only take my accusations as more proof that I didn't like him, or that I thought she'd rushed into the marriage.

I had to remember my nana's adherence to methodology. She would never get two steps of herself. Or go off recipe.

I had to apply that to the case.

Take a deep breath, Rachael.

Think of the facts.

All I had was a photograph. That didn't prove anything.

But it did prove that Marcello knew Pierre. And, from the looks of it, they were close.

Why then has Marcello not shown any grief or sorrow, or even any interest in Pierre's death? The thought sent ice up my spine.

And his marriage to Pippa. It had all happened so suddenly. What were the odds of Marcello turning up in town the day before the murder?

I sat up in bed.

Maybe I should call Jackson.

I had my finger hovering over his name in my phone, just about to press the call button.

I stopped myself. *And tell him what? That I found a picture of two men in my living room?*

He'd probably think I was insane. And I wasn't sure he'd be wrong.

I needed to get some sleep. Maybe things would look clearer in the morning.

***

"Holy..." I started to say as I looked at the time on my phone. 11:00 AM? I hadn't slept that late since I was a teenager. I threw off my blankets and ran into the living room where Pippa and Marcello were still fast asleep on the sofa. I glanced at the boxes of Marcello's items. They were missing something. I reached into my gown and almost cut my fingers on the sharp edges of the photo that seemed to burn a hole there.

"Pippa," I said, shaking her awake and trying to ignore Marcello for a moment while I roused her.

"Huh?" she asked sleepily, rubbing her eyes. "What's going on?"

"It's 11:00 AM! That's what! Who is running the bakery?"

Pippa waved her arm at me and closed her eyes again. "It's cool, it's cool. Branson is there. Don't worry, Rach. I figured we could all use a morning off after last night."

"Aren't you planning on moving this morning?" I said in an urgent whisper.

"I don't think we'll be able to. We might have to stay for another few days, if that's okay."

I sighed. "Fine," I mumbled.

None of this noise seemed to have woken Marcello. He was in a deep sleep that I suspected might have been aided by painkillers the way he was drooling on a cushion. I glanced down at his finger. There seemed to be over a dozen stitches there.

"They saved the finger then?"

Pippa's eyes were still wired shut as she snuggled into the back of him. "Yep," she said. "But they say it's gonna be numb for a while, which might make it hard for him to find work in a cafe or restaurant."

That wouldn't be the only thing holding him back.

Well, now that I had the morning free, I figured it was time to pay a visit to Renee. But as I pulled my jeans and t-shirt on, I felt my energy draining towards that line of inquiry.

The person I really wanted to be investigating was Marcello.

I glanced out the window and was surprised to find that it was gray. From the look of the dark clouds forming in the distance, it was clear that we were in for a summer storm.

I crept out the front door and grabbed an umbrella on my way. I didn't want to wake Pippa. Not before I had decided what to do.

***

The rain had already started by the time I pulled into Renee's driveway, making everything humid and sticky. I'd only been out of the house for fifteen minutes and I already felt as though I needed a shower. And I didn't even want to think about the state of my hair. I just hoped I didn't bump into any handsome men out this way.

"Renee?" I called out through the screen door after I'd knocked and no one had appeared. I could hear the sound of kids running and playing inside, knocking over toys and trampling on each other. I assumed Renee was home and hadn't left five kids to fend for themselves.

But clearly she didn't want to speak to me.

I was just about to leave when I saw a silhouette behind the screen, jolting me a little. My nerves were clearly still shot after the events of the night before.

"Hi there," Renee said quietly. I wondered if she was going to pull the door back, invite me in. The rain was coming down heavy now and I was wearing a rather thin t-shirt.

"I wouldn't be able to come inside, by any chance, would I?"

Renee pulled the door open slowly. She was still wearing that nice floral dress she'd been wearing a few days earlier. It suited her with her new short bob hair cut. "I didn't think you'd want to come inside here," she said softly.

I glanced around the old house. "It's not that bad in here." From the look on her face, I'd clearly misunderstood what she meant. "Sorry, I didn't mean anything."

"I mean, I didn't think you'd want to talk to me after..." Renee stopped talking. "Well, I assume you know what I did?"

I nodded. "I do. That's why I want to talk to you, Renee."

She pulled the door back all the way and sighed gently. "Come in then. I suppose I do owe you an explanation."

Renee pulled some cookies out of a plastic packet and arranged them awkwardly on a plate while I waited for her a few feet away at the dining room table.

"Sorry, this is all I've got," she said, a bit ashamed. "Usually I bake my own fresh, of course. I suppose cookies from a packet don't hold much appeal to you."

I smiled at her. "Usually they would be fine, don't worry. I mean, it's not the packet that's the issue for me. I'm afraid I have been diagnosed with an allergy to gluten."

Renee looked stunned. "But how do you get by with the bakery?"

"I've introduced a lot of gluten-free items," I said, gratefully accepting the tea she placed in front of me.

"So I can at least taste test some of what we are serving."

Renee was quiet for a moment. "When I found out that you had got through the audition ahead of me..." Her voice trailed off and she had to clear her throat before wrapping her own hands around her mug of tea for moral support.

"It's okay," I said. "I'm not here to accuse you. Or judge you. I just want to find out what happened."

"I just saw red," Renee explained, staring down into the depths of her teacup. "I wanted to get through more than anything. You know how much the prize money is, right?"

"Of course." I bit my tongue when I thought about how unlikely it was that any of us there on that day were going to win, though. Even if we'd gotten through—and that was a low chance in itself—then we had to beat twenty-three other bakers, all of them more ruthless than the next, to get right to the end.

Renee waved a hand around her house. "You can see how much that money would have meant to me, and my kids." I could hear them watching TV in the next room, the box temporarily sedating them.

I nodded, feeling guilty now. Maybe I'd never deserved to be cast over Renee. I thought back to Justin and all his quotes and sound bites about what made good TV, but what about the people who really needed the experience? What about the people it could be a matter of life and death for? Was good TV more important than any of that?

"And when Justin let slip that Pierre hadn't actually liked your cake," Renee said, finally looking up at me to cast me a suspicious look. "Well, I just looked at you, young and pretty, and my mind started putting two and two together...even though the answer probably didn't add up."

"I only met him that day," I said quietly.

"I know," Renee said.

"So why did you tell the story to the press then? Were you really that mad at me?"

Renee shook her head. "It was nothing personal, Rachael. The press descended as soon as Pierre was killed, you probably know that. They wanted anything, any little tidbit or gossip from the contestants, and they were willing to pay us for our stories." Renee gulped. "They were offering money. And the juicier the story, the more money they handed out. Even if it had nothing to do with Pierre's actual death."

I sucked in a small breath. Suddenly Renee's outfit and fancy haircut, the ones that didn't quite match the rest of her surroundings, all made sense. "How much did they pay you?"

Renee took a sip of her tea. "Enough." She looked at me. "Let's just say I don't need to win a reality TV show competition anymore." She offered me a weak smile. "I'm sorry, Rachael. But I'm sure you would have done the same thing."

I wasn't sure I would have, but I didn't have five kids under twelve. Under the same circumstances, I probably would have done anything to provide for them. I just nodded. "It's okay. I can handle the rumors, and the gossip. But Renee, I just have to know what happened to Pierre. Did you see anything that day?"

Renee shook her head. "Nothing. I was alone, crying in the green room when it happened."

"And can anyone confirm that?"

She shot me a look. "No. I was alone. But I spoke to Dawn Ashfield soon afterwards. She comforted me. Ask her, she can tell you just how upset I was about the whole thing."

***

So much for not running into any handsome men out this way.

I groaned when I saw the police car pull into the driveway, leaving enough room for my car to get out, but not leaving me enough time to scramble into it to check that my hair looked okay.

"Jackson. I'm surprised to see you here."

He gave me a wry look. "I'm not surprised to see you," he said rather pointedly. But his tone was a little jocular. He cleared his throat. "I hear that you've been poking your nose around?" He raised an eyebrow as he waited for my response.

"And how did you hear about that, exactly?"

"Well, from everyone I interview. Seems you're always there half an hour before I am."

Now it was my turn to raise an eyebrow. "Oh. So I'm there before you, am I?"

He cleared his throat again. "Anyway. I thought you didn't want to help out?"

I didn't say anything.

"Right. You just didn't want to help me out. I see how it is."

I sighed. "YOU didn't want me to help you out, remember?"

"I seem to remember asking for your help."

"No," I said, cutting him off. "You made a point of letting me know that it was Detective Crawford's decision to ask me, not yours."

Jackson's face fell a little. "That's why you refused? Rachael, why do you care if it was Emma's decision or mine?"

I squirmed a little. I didn't really have a good answer for that without revealing the rather shameful truth— that I had been jealous. That I *was* jealous.

"I don't care. I didn't care. I just didn't feel like you really wanted me to help out. That you only asked reluctantly."

"And that matters why? Isn't the only important thing that the case gets solved?"

He was right. It should have been the only important thing. Maybe I'd been foolish, letting my pride get in the way. It was all starting to feel pretty petty now.

"I only started to investigate because my friend—well, he's sort of my friend—Justin was getting the blame, and he wanted me to find out who was really responsible," I explained, lamely. "Honestly, I had no intention of looking into it at all until then."

"Oh, we know all about Justin, don't you worry about that," Jackson replied. His tone was very heated. "We're keeping a very close eye on him."

"Wait, you guys don't think he did it, do you?"

Jackson was quiet for a moment. "You know I can't really share that information with you. But if you've got any information for us that might be useful, I suggest you share it."

"Oh," I said, indignant. "So this is a one way street, is it? I have to tell you everything I know but you can't share anything with me?"

"Yes, Rachael," he replied. "That's how police business works. I wouldn't like to think you were keeping any valuable information from us. Are you?"

I thought about that photo of Marcello with Pierre.

It's not time yet. You don't know anything for sure.

Pippa would kill me.

I shook my head weakly. "No. Only what you already know, I'm sure. I've just talked to Renee and I'm sure you got the same information out of her that I did."

"Well, maybe you ought to come down to the station so we can compare notes and confirm that. After I've interviewed her myself, of course."

"Fine," I said with a sigh. Didn't look like I really had much choice in the matter anyway.

***

The old familiar smell of the Belldale Police Station hit me before I was chaperoned to the interview room. The smell was a stale one, tinged with a shot of melting-plastic and cigarettes, even though it was obviously illegal to smoke inside. Someone had been burning some kind of vanilla oil to try and inject some sweetness into the air.

"I'm sure Renee didn't do it," I said, even before I'd sat down in the old familiar seat of the interview room. "I can tell you that right away. You don't need to look at my notes." Mostly because I didn't have any and I was worried he might actually want to see physical proof of my hunches.

I wondered if I kept at this investigation game, whether I would have to start taking notes like a real detective. But that would be sort of like committing to it. And I still wasn't sure I was quite there yet.

Jackson shifted uncomfortably as he settled across from me, in a far more comfortable, padded seat. "What makes you say that? How can you be so sure that Renee is innocent?" I analyzed his tone. It didn't sound like he didn't believe me, necessarily, just that he was eager to know what evidence I had.

I shrugged. "She only wanted to go on the TV show for the money. She has that now. So she has no reason to want Pierre dead."

"You mean the money she got from the press?"

I slunk back in my seat. Jackson knew about the rumors. Of course he did.

He continued, "But she wouldn't have known she had that when she committed the murder. Hypothetically, of course."

Good point.

I quickly ran through what Renee had told me, before filling him in on everything I knew about Adam Ali and Justin as well.

Jackson nodded slowly. "Those are our three main suspects then?"

"Do you mean they are the cop's three suspects when you say *our*? Or do you just use it to refer to me?"

He still wasn't giving much away. If he'd just accidentally let something important slip in a moment of weakness then he wasn't going to admit to it.

I sighed. "Yes. Those are the three suspects."

Jackson leaned back and the front two legs of his chair raised off the floor a little. He examined me closely.

"And you're sure you don't know anything else that you're not telling us? There's no secret suspect up your sleeve?"

I shook my head. "Why would you even ask that? I've told you everything I know. I've told you about everyone I suspect might have killed Pierre."

"Because if you are keeping something from us, Rachael, that would be a very serious matter."

I bit down hard on my tongue. It was about to spill out: *Marcello did it!*

But I just shook my head. "Looks like I'm not that much more competent than you are right now."

Jackson leaned forward suddenly in his chair, bringing the top two legs down with a thud. "I think we're done here."

Chapter 10

At least Marcello couldn't cause any trouble while he was asleep. It was my preferred state for him.

But Pippa awoke as I approached the sofa. It was already 10:00 AM of the newly appointed 'moving day' and I knew she'd appreciate the suggestion I was about to put forth.

"How about I move the boxes for you guys? Go on ahead and you can catch up with me later. I know that Marcello can't do much with his finger all stitched up like that," I said, swinging a look towards Marcello's index finger that still looked liked a swollen sausage that had been badly stitched up. "And you ought to stay here to look after him, don't you think?" I added, trying to sound sympathetic.

Pippa nodded a little hesitantly. "Only if you're sure though, Rach."

"Couldn't be more sure."

With the boxes loaded in the back of my car and the keys to Pippa's new apartment firmly in the pocket of my jeans, I was all set...for the chance to snoop through all of Marcello's stuff.

Sure, I felt a little bit guilty for lying to Pippa, but it was all going to be worth it when I found proof, undeniable proof, that Marcello had known Pierre Hamilton and had been there the day he was killed.

It took even longer than I'd feared to get to Pippa's new place in downtown Belldale. Looked like she was soon to be no closer than a twenty-five minute drive away from me. Right now, she was a twenty-five second walk away from me.

That was if she still wanted to go ahead with the moving plans.

I had an inkling that once I found what I had a hunch I'd find, her plans might change somewhat.

When I finally pulled into her new place, I barely had time to even appreciate how nice the apartment was.

If this was located anywhere else, say on the other side of the highway, I'd live here, I thought, as I hurried in with the boxes. I wanted to be inside, out of the way of preying eyes, before I unleashed the carnage.

Using the same knife that Marcello had used to slice through his finger, I began to gut the boxes, one by one. I had no idea how long it would be before Pippa, and maybe even Marcello himself, joined me.

Items spilled out as I sliced the boxes open. I got down to my knees and sifted through them, looking for something, anything, that would confirm the unthinkable: that Marcello had killed Pierre.

It was a mad scramble at first and I realized I was getting nowhere the way I was chucking things over my shoulder and frantically sifting through books, photos, receipts, and random accessories.

I took a deep breath and thought about what my nana would have told me. "Take your time, Rachael. Be methodical. Don't leave anything to chance."

I started over and began to sort the items into piles, taking the time to check over each one carefully.

"There has to be something here."

Time passed without me realizing it as I flicked through Marcello's journals and diaries and passport. Most of the writing was in Italian and anything I couldn't read, I secretively placed in my purse to take with me—either to show to someone who spoke Italian, or to translate it later myself with the help of Professor Google.

I was just about to pack everything up and send Pippa a text when something came fluttering out of one of Marcello's leather backed journals.

A bus ticket.

Innocuous enough at first, I turned it over and read the details.

I froze. It was a ticket for a concession pass to Hillsville Park. The place that played host to the *Baking Warriors* audition and the makeshift studio on audition day.

My heart almost stopped beating. I even reached up and thumped my chest to try and get it working again. With my hands shaking now, I checked the dates.

Then double-checked them.

July 22nd. The day of the auditions. The day that Pierre Hamilton had died.

I was so shocked that I didn't hear the footsteps enter the empty apartment behind me. I probably wouldn't have heard an earthquake in that moment.

I probably wouldn't have heard *Marcello* in that moment.

But it wasn't him that entered the apartment. It was Pippa. And it was too late for me to hide the wreckage.

I spun around as I saw the shadow behind me.

"Rachael?" Pippa's voice said. "What the heck are you doing?"

***

I scrambled to my feet, trying to hide the evidence of what I was doing by kicking the exposed items underneath an overturned cardboard box. I shoved the ticked into my coat pocket.

I gulped. "Pippa, it's not what it looks like." Even though it kind of was exactly what it looked like.

"Why are you snooping through Marcello's stuff?" At first Pippa's face was nothing but confusion, but all color and expression drained from it as the realization dawned upon her.

"What? Rachael, please tell me there's another reason why you are going through Marcello's things." Her voice was a breathy whisper now. "Please tell me that, I don't know, that you're secretly obsessed with him or something! Or secretly in love with him. Anything would be better... Anything but...but..." She couldn't even finish her sentence.

"Pippa, I didn't want to tell you until I was certain..."

Pippa shook her head and backed away from me, tripping over a box as she went. She barely even noticed as she straightened herself up.

"Marcello knew Pierre, Pippa."

"No, he didn't," she whispered furiously. "Don't be stupid."

"He did. He was at the studio that day, Pippa."

But she didn't want to listen to me. "Big deal, what does that prove? So what, he was at the studio." But her eyes were wild and her voice shook.

Pippa crossed her arms over her chest like a petulant child. "You're only saying all of this because you don't like Marcello. You think I made a mistake by marrying him."

"Pippa, I have proof," I said, turning over the box to find the bus ticket. "Here, look at this," I said, waving it in her face. But she turned away and stuck her nose up like I had poked a dish of sour milk underneath her nose.

Pippa was still backing away from me while my arm was outstretched, the ticket still dangling from it.

"I can't believe this, Rachael. I thought you liked Marcello!" She stamped her foot on the floor this time, becoming more and more like a four year old by the second. "Did you only volunteer to help move his stuff so that you could come up with this crazy theory?"

I dropped the arm holding the bus ticket. Time to try a different tactic.

"When did you meet Marcello, Pippa?" I asked gently.

"What does that matter?" Pippa asked, but some of the insolence was gone from her voice and she looked up at me plaintively.

"Pippa, when you met him, did you tell him where you were from? Who you lived with? Anything like that?"

Pippa shook her head tearfully. "I guess so," she said, as tears dropped to the ground. "I told him I was from Belldale, of course, and he was so excited to get married and move here. Or at least, I thought he wanted to move here." She sucked in a sharp breath. "Maybe he just wanted to come here to..."

I hugged Pippa tight to me. "It's okay. You'll be safe now. You don't have to worry. I'll call Jackson." I just hoped it wasn't too late.

"It can't be true, Rach." Pippa's lip started to tremble. She slumped down onto the floor and looked around the empty apartment before bursting into tears, her whole body shaking while a horrible noise that sounded like a dying animal escaped from her lungs.

"Pippa, it's okay," I said, hurrying towards her, but she pushed me away. It wasn't so much a case of shooting the messenger as it was of shoving the messenger onto the floor.

"Pippa, please."

"I thought he loved me," she sobbed, burying her head in her knees as she rocked back and forth. "But all this time he was only using me."

"Pippa, please." I knelt down besides her and tried to place my arm round her shoulders.

"I should have known that someone as handsome as him would never be interested in someone like me," she wailed.

"Pippa, that's not true. Of course they would be. It's just Marcello specifically that wasn't."

Her wailing only grew louder. Okay, that was a stupid thing to say.

"I'm calling him right now!" Pippa lifted her head and searched frantically for her phone.

"Pippa, wait, I'm not sure that's such a good idea."

But she climbed to her feet and pushed me away. She already had Marcello on the other end of the line before I could stop her.

"I know what you did, Marcello! I know that you killed Pierre!" she shrieked. "How could I ever have been so stupid as to marry you? I never want to see you again!" She shouted, before adding, "And I don't suppose I will, now that you are going to be in prison for the rest of your life!"

She hung up and threw the phone across the room. "Pippa, I don't think that was a very good idea."

The phone was already smashed into a hundred pieces. Along with all the other wreckage, it fit right in.

Pippa looked at the mess and burst into tears. "Oh, it looks like Marcello has been here!" She sobbed in a weird mixture of sorrow and affection. I raced over and gave her a hug.

"We have to go though, Pippa. And I need to call Jackson right away."

***

The police car was already waiting out the front of my apartment as I quickly pulled into the driveway, my brakes letting out an ear-piercing screech as I pulled to a stop.

I raced up the driveway towards Jackson, who was exiting the front door, suspiciously empty handed.

Jackson just glared at me. "He's gone, Rachael. Marcello is gone."

Chapter 11

Two Months Later.

The stale smell of burnt plastic and cigarette smoke hit me.

I had something I needed to do that morning. Before my life—possibly? hopefully?—changed that afternoon.

"Is Detective Whitaker here?"

He led me into the interview room.

"You look awfully dressed up," Jackson said when he entered. "Off on a hot date?"

I'd gotten a brand new haircut and added a burgundy tint to my brunette hair. And I'd splurged on a new outfit.

"Not exactly." I shifted uncomfortably. "Jackson, I just wanted to make things right with us again."

He glanced around to make sure the door was securely shut. "You're just lucky you aren't in any more trouble than you already are."

"So you won't accept my apology then?"

"You shouldn't have kept that information from us, Rachael. Now Marcello's on the run and we might never have a chance to catch him. An apology hardly cuts it."

I was frustrated. "You mean someone else might catch him? A cop from a different jurisdiction or different state, making you look bad?" I asked. "That's what this is really all about, isn't it? I came to you as soon as I had proof. You're just being stubborn. Refusing to take my calls for two months straight. This is personal, not professional."

Jackson just shook his head and looked away. But I knew I was right.

"I have to go," I said quietly. "It's an important day."

***

Pippa had barely moved from her spot on the sofa in two months.

"It's okay, Rach. I won't stay here forever." Her hand draped over one side of the sofa as she reached for a packet of supermarket cookies that were lying on the floor. They'd been left open over night and as she listlessly bit into one, there was no crunch. "I prefer them this way," she said in her usual zombie-like voice before she continued to munch on it with her eyes glossed over.

I was hoping that Pippa wouldn't stay there forever, but far more for her sake than for mine. This depression had gone on long enough and it was threatening to suck her under and never let go of her.

"Well, wish me luck," I said lamely as I waved my car keys in the air.

"Huh?" Pippa turned her glassy eyes towards me, confused.

"It's the do-over of the auditions today. Remember?"

"Oh." Pippa brightened just a little and put down her cookie. "Break a leg, Rachael."

***

Justin had obviously had a mini-makeover of his own sometime during the past two months. His dark hair was now long and floppy and his new bangs sported a stripe of bright blue.

"Rachael!" he exclaimed brightly before racing over to give me a hug inside the Hillsville Park studios. It was a bit eerie being back there. Justin seemed genuinely pleased to see me and I had to admit I felt a bit of warmth towards him as well. Maybe absence really did make the heart grow fonder.

"Can you believe all this?" he said, breaking the embrace. "I still can't believe it myself. Is that guy still on the run? Have you heard anything?" Justin asked, bringing a hand up to his chest.

I shook my head. "I'm kind of on the outs with the police department."

Justin let out a loud, dramatic sigh. "I'm just glad I'M off the hook for the whole thing. And I guess I've got you to thank for that."

"I guess so. Have you seen Adam since it all happened?"

Justin rolled his eyes. "Only once. This morning. He's being a total nightmare, as per usual. Don't know what I ever saw in that guy." He flicked his bangs out of his face dramatically in a way that reminded me of Adam.

"He's here then?" I asked. "And Renee?"

"Both of them are back for another round of torture," Justin said, looking down at his trusty tablet. "Speaking of, Renee is up first. I've got to go track her down."

It surprised me that Renee had turned up to audition again. She'd said that the blood money from the gossip sites had been almost as much the prize money from the show.

I supposed she could always do with *more* money. Who couldn't? Still, something about it didn't sit right with me.

I was still mulling it over when I heard a familiar voice.

"Rachael!" Dawn said warmly as she practically skipped over to me. I was so happy to see her. "Oh, I'm so glad to see you made it back." She gave me a comforting hug that helped to soothe my nerves as I took in a breath of her lavender perfume. "Do you have five minutes? Come join me in my dressing room for a coffee?"

"I think I might have to go with herbal tea," I said, worried that the coffee wouldn't be great for my already shot nerves.

"Herbal tea it is then."

I started to follow her into her room when I heard heavy footsteps running after me.

"Rachael, where do you think you're going." Justin started to admonish me, but his tone softened when he saw I was with a guest of honor. "Oh, hello, Dawn," he said with an awkward little curtsy. "I just need to have a quick word with Rachael," he said with a sickly sweet smile. "You don't mind, do you?"

Dawn shot me a look before giving Justin her blessing. "I'll wait for you in my dressing room," Dawn said.

"I'll be calling for you in fifteen, Rachael," Justin said sternly. "Make sure you're ready. The new judge Colin Evans is an even harder taskmaster than Pierre was, if you can believe it, and he WON'T wait for you. Got it?" He clucked his tongue. "I've got your gluten-free cheesecake all ready for them to taste." He stopped and scrolled through his tablet. "It was chocolate, right?"

"Peanut butter," I corrected him.

"Right. It will be ready. Just make sure you are. Right, Rachael? You got it?"

I nodded firmly. "Got it."

***

"Oh shoot," Dawn said just as she'd poured the hot water into my teacup. "I've got to be ready to start filming in five minutes or Justin is going to skin me alive." She chuckled. "Why don't you wait here and finish your tea?" Dawn patted my knee while I settled into her comfy suede sofa. "You deserve a rest after everything you've been through."

I gratefully accepted the offer as she tottered off, but it was hard to relax knowing that the clock was counting down and Justin was waiting.

I decided not to cut it too fine. Ten minutes before my call time, I picked up my coat and walked to the door.

"Just where do you think you are going?"

Renee pushed me back into the room and locked the door before I could comprehend what was happening.

"Renee!" I shouted. "Are you kidding me?" I kicked against the door, figuring it was a joke and expecting that she would be back to let me out in a few seconds.

But she didn't return. "Renee?" I called again, more frantically this time.

"Let me out!" I screamed, banging on the wall. "You can't keep me locked in here!"

I was starting to panic.

Oh, this cannot be happening.

Renee really does have it out for me.

Then, a shock of ice ran down my spine.

What if I'd been wrong about Marcello?

I could hear my name being called over the loudspeaker. I looked down at my phone desperately. No reception. I banged on the door again. Geez, those doors were thick.

"JUSTIN!" I screamed. My phone might not have had any reception, but it was still capable of keeping the time. And letting me know that three minutes of my allowed audition time had already dripped away. If I didn't get out of there, like, immediately, I was going to miss my already tiny window.

Window.

I glanced over at the far side of the dressing room. It was tiny. But that wasn't the only problem. The one small window was at least seven feet off the ground.

The sofa wouldn't budge the first time I yanked at it. I stood up and took a deep breath, trying to figure out how to go about it logically. I ran around to the other side and pushed, rather than pull, putting all my weight behind me as I pushed off with my knees, lunging towards the grey monolith.

I winced, looking down at the expensive suede, which I was sure was not meant to be climbed on. But this was an emergency.

Right before I was about to pull myself up towards the window, I glanced back at the spot where the sofa had been.

Sitting there, right in the middle of the floor, was a brown-colored cheesecake. It had been hidden under the lounge chair.

"What the heck," I said, jumping off the sofa and running over to the cake sitting on the floor. I leaned over and sniffed it. The smell was unmistakable. It was definitely peanut butter.

I looked at the crumbly crust. It was unmistakably gluten-free.

It was definitely my cake.

I just sat there on my knees, staring at it for a minute in complete confusion.

Why does Dawn have my cheesecake in her room?

And what cake were the judges going to taste?

My heart skipped a beat when I remembered what Justin had said. "It's chocolate, isn't it?"

The realization hit me.

They're not eating my cake! They're eating a tampered cake.

I stood up and quickly began to pace. On that day, my first audition, Dawn had never eaten my cake. And Wendy had only pretended to, having eaten the 'real' cake before the auction even took place.

Only Pierre had eaten the cake.

It wasn't Marcello who had killed Pierre. Or Adam. Or Renee. Or even Justin.

It was Dawn.

And now she was going to kill someone else.

The loudspeaker crackled and the next name was called out.

I'd missed my chance.

I just hoped I still had time to save a life.

Chapter 12

I banged and banged on the door and finally it opened, causing me to stumble forward face first as I almost ended up on the ground.

"I'm sorry," Renee said politely as she smoothed down her dress. "It was nothing personal, Rachael. I just couldn't have you doing your audition. They are only going to cast one woman from Belldale and it HAS to be me."

So she was as cutthroat as ever.

"It doesn't matter," I gasped, pushing past her. "I just need to get to the audition room. Do you know if anyone has eaten my cake?"

I was sprinting breathlessly towards the audition room while Renee chased over me. "No," she called out. "You never auditioned, so why would they?"

Good point. I paused just for a second to catch my breath. "You might have inadvertently saved a life by locking me in that room, Renee." I reached out and placed my hands on her shoulders for support, while she shot me a horrified look.

"What are you talking about?"

"We have to go! Who knows what other cakes she has poisoned. Come on, let's go!"

**

I burst into the room.

"Put that cake down! It could kill you!"

"Rachael, what the heck are you doing?"

I turned to see Adam's stricken face. So, it was his audition. "Erm." I swallowed. "Sorry, Adam. It's nothing personal."

I turned my attention back to the three-story wedding cake sitting on the judge's table. "BUT DO NOT EAT THAT CAKE."

"Oh, Rachael!" Adam said, pushing me out of the way. "Do you always have to ruin everything for me?"

"I'm sorry, Adam," I said, bringing down the only weapon I had, my purse, to smash the wedding cake.

Adam shrieked. "How could you?"

I stood back and looked at the wreckage, and at Dawn's crumpled face behind it. Her ashen expression told me everything I needed to know.

"I'm sorry, Adam," I whispered. "I had to do it. Even if it wasn't poisoned, that cake was a travesty."

***

"Please," I pleaded with Jackson. "I know you're not talking to me, but just let me have one minute to speak to Dawn before you take her away. Haven't I at least earned that?"

He sighed reluctantly before he pulled Dawn around to face me, her hands still handcuffed behind her. Jackson turned his face away in a futile effort to give us some privacy.

"Just tell me, Dawn. Why did you do it?" I tried to keep the shaking out of my voice. Tried to hide the hurt over my surrogate nana betraying me like that.

"I was about to be replaced on the program." Dawn turned her head towards the studio and let out a bitter laugh. "I wasn't making good TV, as they say," she murmured, her voice suddenly sounding like it was coming from so far away.

"But what did Pierre have to do with it?"

"Pierre Hamilton was the executive producer. It was all his decision." Dawn turned back to face me. "Do you know how long I waited, sidelined to pathetic morning shows for decades, overlooked and underappreciated, just waiting for my one shot at fame? After years of scratching and clawing my way into a primetime position, I wasn't going to let anyone take that away from me. Certainly not Pierre Hamilton," she spat. "And not this new guy either. Colin Evans wasn't going to take my job away from me either."

"No. You did that to yourself. Did you have to use my cake to do it, though?"

Dawn offered me an apologetic smile. "I'm sorry, my dear. It was nothing personal."

I took a step back and nodded at Jackson. "You can take her away," I whispered.

In the end, the producers selected two contestants from Belldale to appear on the next season of *Baking Warriors*.

And I wasn't either of them.

***

The flight was late, but I had a feeling Pippa would have waited a million years for that plane to land.

"Marcello!" Pippa screamed, running so fast that her legs were nothing but a blur underneath her. "I can't believe it!" she gasped, flinging herself into his arms.

I hurried after her, keen to see the happy reunion. Eager to see that Marcello was in one piece. I mean, it was Marcello. Maybe the best we could hope for with him was several pieces.

"But why did you run away, sweetheart? When you knew you didn't do it?" Tears were flowing down Pippa's face.

"I couldn't live like that, with you thinking that I did it, that I was guilty," Marcello said. "I knew how it would have looked as well, with my reputation for accidents. I knew everyone must think I could do such a stupid thing. All I would have to do would be walk past a cake and accidentally poison it." Marcello pulled away from Pippa for a second and looked at me.

"I was such a big fan of the show and Pierre. I met him years ago and got that photo." He stopped to collect himself. "I went along to the audition thinking I might get on the show. Of course I didn't, but I didn't want to tell Pippa where I had been that day because I'd told her I was out looking for a job." He turned back to Pippa. "I'm so sorry, my darling."

"No, Marcello, don't say that. I'm so sorry, baby," Pippa said as Marcello wrapped her hands in his. "I should never have doubted you."

Marcello kissed her hands and told her it was all right, that none of that mattered anymore. "Just as long as we're back together now."

I watched them for a moment and I could see that they were genuinely happy and in love. And even though Marcello could break just about anything, I knew their relationship was one thing he would make sure he'd keep together.

"Come on, you two," I said, laughing. "We've got a wedding reception to organize."

Epilogue

Three months later

"You look beautiful, Pippa," I said as she carefully examined her dress in the door of the silver fridge, which was serving as a mirror. We were standing in the kitchen of the bakery, about to make our big appearance in the reception area.

"It's not too 'wedding-y,' is it?" She turned to me, concerned. "It's not too 'bridal'?"

"Um." I looked at the bright purple dress that perfectly matched her hair. "No, I don't think it's too bridal. I don't think I've ever seen a bride wearing anything like that." I walked over and gave her a kiss on the cheek. "I do think it's just perfect for you, though."

We laughed, and danced, and made sure we ate every bite of wedding cake under Adam's watchful eye. He was recently back from shooting the show but had signed a strict confidentiality contract, so he couldn't tell us how far he'd gotten.

From the way he'd hounded Pippa into letting him cater the reception, I had a suspicion he'd been eliminated in the first round.

"I still can't believe I paid for this," Pippa said, shaking her head as she nibbled at the thick almond icing. "Rach, you really need to expand into the wedding cake market."

"Shh!" I said, and we both giggled.

"Well, should we call an early end to this wedding reception?" Pippa asked me with a wink after a few more spins around the dance floor.

"What? Why?"

Pippa pointed at the clock. "It's almost 7:30."

"And?"

She gave me a 'you've got to be kidding me look.' "Don't you know what it's the premiere of tonight?"

I threw my head back with a little groan. "No, Pippa. I don't want to see it."

"Come on," she said, linking her arm through mine. "Let's find a TV."

***

I didn't manage to pull my face out of my hands for even a second during my 'audition' scene, which was part of a tribute to Pierre that aired at the start of the program. But the sound of my voice and my stuttering over my words was more than enough to make me want to die.

"I can't believe they kept that in there," I groaned.

"They must have thought it made good TV."

Pippa, Marcello, and I were all squeezed onto the couch together, huddled round the TV set. They kept telling me they were going to get their own place soon, but there was no rush.

All during the episode, I kept reliving my on-screen debut in my head, meaning I barely paid attention to what was actually happening on the screen. It was all a bur of icing sugar and chocolate and tears and Adam flailing about dramatically, posing for the camera every time it came near him.

I was wrong. Adam DID make it through the first episode.

"Tune in next week when disaster strikes one unlucky contestant," the voice over said ominously.

"Is it sabotage?" The camera zoomed in on a slow motion shot of Renee, who was found surreptitiously tampering with what appeared to be Adam's cake mix.

"The most evil contestant we've ever seen on *Baking Warriors*," the booming voice shouted as the special effects turned Renee's eyes red.

I rolled my eyes. She was only adding an extra teaspoon of sugar to Adam's mixture.

"I'm glad I got out when I did, though," I stated. "I just wouldn't have made good TV."

Thank You!

Thanks for reading *Death by Chocolate Cake*. I hope you enjoyed reading the story as much as I enjoyed writing it. If you did, it would be awesome if you left a review for me on Amazon and/or Goodreads.

If you would like to know about all my new releases and have the opportunity to get free books, make sure you sign up for our Cozy Mystery Newsletter.

FairfieldPublishing.com/cozy-newsletter

On the next page, I have included a preview of my first book, *A Pie to Die For*. If you haven't read it yet, be sure to pick up a copy

I am also including a preview of the first cozy mystery from my friend Miles Lancaster. I really hope you like it!

Stacey Alabaster

Preview: A Pie to Die For

I let out a little squeal as I brushed the foul, winged creature aside. "Not today buddy, not today!" I watched it intently as it flew away, a tiny black dot disappearing into the fall sky, and was glad that I hadn't needed to swat the poor thing. I heaved a sigh of relief as I took the lids off my desserts and a sweet cloud of vanilla, chocolate, and coffee bean, all mixed together, hit my nostrils.

That was the danger of serving food outdoors: flies. I was hoping that I'd seen the last of them for the day. Normally, I had my cakes and pastries sequestered safely away in my bakery, Rachael's Boutique Cakes. But today, being outside was a necessary evil. It was the annual Belldale Street Fair and it was my last chance to show the town that my cakes were worth stopping for, my last chance to save my failing bakery and keep the bank from serving me an eviction notice.

My fingers trembled as I removed the last of the lids and rearranged the decorations on my stall. I'd chosen a pink and white theme for the day and I piled cupcakes and macaroons high on a cute little pink cake stand, trying not to drop them with my shaking hands.

Meanwhile, I watched the numerous employees of the Bakermatic food tent set up their factory made cakes with soldier-like intensity. My stomach dropped as I saw a sign go up with "Free Samples" written on it.

I glanced at my own price tags. How was I ever going to compete with free samples? Slowly, I reached over and, with a black marker, slashed my prices in half.

It was going to be a long day.

***

Midday. Three hours into the fair and I'd had a total of four customers. Meanwhile, the Bakermatic tent a hundred feet away was bursting at the seams with people trying to claim their free samples, which never seemed to run out.

Maybe I should just pack up and take the cakes back to the store.

I saw a figure out of the corner of my eye waddling towards the stall.

Oh no, not this woman, I thought. The lady, middle-aged with cat-eyed spectacles and a streak of pink in the front of her otherwise brown hair, only ever seemed to come into my bakery for the sole purpose of tutting and telling me that my cakes were twice the price of the cakes and pastries that Bakermatic sold.

"But that's because mine are twice as good." I would try to reason with her, only to be met with a sharp lift of her eyebrows.

"I use quality ingredients. And I pay my staff a proper wage." After I would tell her that, I'd lean back with my arms crossed over my chest. She could hardly argue with paying people—students, single mothers—a living wage, right? Wrong. She always tutted and stuck up her nose before informing me, loudly, that she was going to take her business to Bakermatic instead. "I can get a coffee AND a cupcake there for the price of just a cupcake here!"

And it seemed like half the town followed her. Every day, more and more customers chose their low prices over my painfully handcrafted selection of cookies, cupcakes, and pastries. Thus the ever growing pile of bills on my kitchen table. And I thought going into business for myself at age twenty-five was going to be glamorous.

Now she was here. I bristled as she approached with bull-like intensity, her eyes focused on my table, waiting for her to cast more disparaging comments. She pointed to a fresh baked pie on my table. "I'll have a slice of that."

My face stretched into a wide smile. "Really?"

Her coin purse paused in midair. "Are you trying to turn away a customer?"

"No, of course not! Just surprised that you would want a piece of my pie. What with Bakermatic giving away free samples down the road."

She screwed her face up. "Don't worry! I'll be sampling theirs as well!" She threw my pie a look of disdain. "It's for my food blog. I've got to try something from every stall. So don't go getting a big head, thinking that I'd choose you over them!"

Of course not. "Your blog?" I watched eagerly as she sampled my pie. "Well, surely you'll have to give my pie a better review than Bakermatic's, despite the price. Mine are fresh, made from all local ingredients, all hand-made every day."

She cut me off and slammed the plate down on the table before scribbling something in her notebook. "I will be taking cost into account as well, don't you worry about that, young lady. I still don't know how you can get away with charging an arm and a leg for this!"

She picked up her piece of pie with disdain and walked away—heading straight for the Bakermatic stand. I stood there with my mouth hanging open before I remembered I was supposed to be attracting customers, not repelling them. I tightened my apron and put on my brightest smile as a man with ginger hair and a portly waist line hurried past.

"Hey!" I said, throwing him my best flirtatious smile as I tried to usher him back to my stand. "You gotta try one of these."

He screwed his nose up. "I think I'll try one from Bakermatic instead." He patted his oversized tummy before adding, "Gotta watch the calories, you know. I can't have too many."

"But mine are made from all natural ingredients." Ahhh, it was too late. He was already waddling towards the Bakermatic stand, like they needed one more customer to add to the overflowing mob already crowding their tent.

I sighed. What was the use? How could I compete with thousands of free samples? This street fair was supposed to be my way to attract more customers, to get the word out that I had the best baked goods in town, and I couldn't even get anyone to stop and try them.

"Hey there," a kind voice called out. "Why are you looking so sad for?"

I glanced up. There he was. Tall, dark floppy hair. I guessed he was about five years older than me, which was just about perfect. Five years older and five inches taller.

A grin swept over my face in spite of myself. "Nothing," I said hurriedly, scurrying to tidy all the rows of unsold cakes and pies. Must look professional. Must look successful.

"Aww come on," he said, with a smile that brightened the damp day. "A gorgeous girl like you, with cakes that look so good. What's got you down so bad?"

I sighed. "That's very kind of you to say. But even though my cakes might look good," I brushed over his compliment about my own appearance. "it doesn't mean they're selling." I pointed down the road to the line that snaked out of the Bakermatic tent. "I think they've got the monopoly on baked goods."

"Ah, I've heard about them." He nodded slowly and pursed his lips. "They're supposed to be evil, right?"

"Pure evil." I raised my eyebrows and let out a little

laugh.

"Well, I'd rather try one of yours."

He cast me a lingering look that made the butterflies in my stomach take flight. I perused the table, trying to find the best piece for him. I settled on my delicate carrot cake with cream cheese frosting and little red heart-shaped dots sprinkled on top. *Too much?* I told myself I'd explain that I hadn't noticed the hearts if he pointed them out.

He took the cake and—was it my imagination?—smiled a little when he saw the heart-shaped sprinkles. "Very nice," he said before opening his mouth wide.

It was a nervous few seconds before he gave his verdict.

"Perfect." He dusted off his hands and nodded. "If all your cakes are this good, I think I'll be seeing you again very soon. Rachael, wasn't it?" He nodded at the shop sign name.

"That's me." I grinned. "And you are?"

"Jackson. I'll be seeing you again soon, Rachael."

As I watched him walk away, I grinned to myself, my stomach warm and gooey as a cupcake fresh from the oven. Maybe today wasn't such a disaster after all.

***

I kicked off my heels. As soon as I sat down there was a knock on the door. Great timing.

But I grinned when I saw Pippa's shock of red curls peaking through the windows. After the day I'd had, I'd forgotten what day it was. Time for Criminal Point.

Pippa had her hair tucked under a baseball cap wearing the logo of a company I didn't recognize. She threw it off and it rolled under one of my designer chairs. "How did it go today?"

I held my hands up. "I don't even want to talk about it." Not even the cute stranger, although that was the kind of thing I usually shared with Pippa. But talking about Mr. Handsome was going to mean dredging up all the other junk: the unsold cakes, the bills piling up at the door, the imminent eviction notice. I slumped back onto the sofa.

"All I want to do is lie here, tune out, and watch some TV."

"What's on the box tonight?"

I grinned at her. "Pippa, you know very well what

night it is."

She stuck her tongue out. "Shall I order the pizza?"

I nodded gratefully. "Pepperoni thin crust! You know the deal. We always order the same thing."

***

Five minutes of Criminal Point left to go. The on screen detectives had just reached that point where the light bulb goes off and they were about to burst through the door of the final suspect, the one who had committed the murder.

Pippa and I leaned over, breaths held, pizza cheese dripping onto our plate below. Just as they were about to reveal the killer, the broadcast was interrupted for an "Important Local News Update."

"Nooo!" I squealed, reaching for the remote, stabbing at it randomly as though I could bring the program back to life. "What happened!"

"Shh," Pippa said. I felt her nails dig into my bicep. "Listen!" Pippa hissed for me to be quiet.

"What?"

"Shh!"

I dropped my pizza as a shot of the street fair flashed onto the screen. My mouth dropped as the anchor, a woman with a helmet of blonde hair and a stern face, delivered the news. "A woman has died following the Belldale Annual Street Fair, and police suspect that foul play may have been at work. They are investigating suspects now, and are urging anyone with details to come forward." An image of the victim flashed onto the box. Middle-aged, brown hair with a pink streak down the front. Her name was Colleen Batters.

Pippa and I stared to look at each other. "I know that woman!"

Pippa gulped. "How? Rachael, please tell me you just know her from your book club or something?"

I shook my head. "I served her today. Oh, Pippa! She was one of the few people to actually eat at my stand!" My heart started thumping and my head felt like it was pumped full of helium. Had I killed Colleen? My mind started fumbling back through the day's events, to all the other people who'd eaten my food. What about that cute guy? Jackson. Was he okay?

There was a knock on the door. I was too stunned to even stand up so Pippa bounced over and pulled it open.

A voice on the other side cleared his throat. "I'm looking for a Miss Robison."

Pippa turned slowly to look at me. "It's a cop," she mouthed in an exaggerated way with her eyes popped.

I walked over to the door like a zombie.

There he was. "Jackson?"

He cleared his throat again. "Officer Whitaker actually, under these circumstances. Miss Robinson, I'm afraid I need you to come in and answer a few questions. You're under suspicion for the murder of Mrs. Colleen Batters."

Thanks for reading a sample of *A Pie to Die For* I really hope you liked it.

Stacey Alabaster

Preview: Murder in the Mountains

Screams were not a normal part of the workday at Aspen Breeze. When Jennifer heard the anguished cry of the maid, she ran around the desk and sprinted out the door. Clint, not through with his breakfast, followed at her heels. The door to the room had been left open. The maid stood on the thick burgundy carpet in front of the unmade bed and pointed at the hot tub.

Water remained in the tub, but it wasn't swirling. The occupant, a red-haired, slightly chubby man whose name Jennifer had forgotten, was face down. His blue running shorts had changed to a darker blue due to dampness. Reddish colorations marred his throat. Another dark spot of blood mixed with hair around his right temple. Pale red splotches marred the water.

For a moment, she felt like the ground had opened and she had fallen into blackness. Legs weakened. Knees buckled. She shook her head and a few incoherent syllables came from her mouth. Clint's arm grasped her around her waist.

"Step back. It's okay," he said.

It was a silly thing to say, he later thought. Clearly, it was not okay, but in times of stress people will often say and do stupid things.

He eased her backward, and then sat her down on the edge of the bed. He walked back and took a second look at the hot tub. He had seen dead bodies when he covered the police beat. It wasn't a routine occurrence, but he had stood in the rain twice and on an asphalt pavement once as EMTs covered a dead man and lifted him into an ambulance.

By the time he turned around, Jennifer was back on her feet and the color had returned to her cheeks.

She patted her maid on the shoulder. "Okay, it's all right. We have to call the police. You can go, Maria. Go to the office and lay down."

"Yes, ma'am."

She glanced at Clint and saw he had his cell phone out.

"...at the Aspen Breeze Lodge," he was saying. "There's a dead body in Unit Nine. It doesn't look like it was a natural death." He nodded then slipped the cell phone in his pocket. "They said the chief was out on a call but should be here within fifteen minutes."

"Good." Jennifer put her hands on her hips. Her gaze stared toward the hot tub. A firm, determined tone came back in her voice.

"Clint, those marks on his throat. The red on his forehead. This wasn't an accident, was it?"

"We can't really say for sure. He might have tripped and hit...." The words withered in the face of her laser stare. "I doubt it. I...I really can't say for sure but...I doubt it."

They looked at one another for a few seconds. Light yellow flames rose up from the artificial fireplace and the crackling of wood sounded from the flames. Jennifer sighed. She realized there was nothing to do except wait for the police.

The silence was interrupted by a tall, thin man, unshaven as yet, who rushed in.

"Bill, what are you doing with the door open? It's still cold...." He stopped as if hit by a stun gun. Eyes widened. He stumbled but caught himself before he fell to the carpeted floor. "Oh, no! What happened?"

Jennifer shifted into her professional tone as manager. "We don't know yet, sir. I assume you knew this man."

He nodded weakly. "Yeah, Bill's been a friend of mine for years."

"I remember you from when you checked in yesterday, but I'm sorry I can't remember your name."

"Dale Ramsey."

Ramsey had a thin, pale face that flashed even paler. There was a chair close to him and he collapsed in it. He had an aquiline nose and chin but curly brown hair. His hand went to his heart.

"Sorry you had to learn about your friend's death this way, Mr. Ramsey," Jennifer said. "I regret to say I've forgotten his name too."

"Bill Hamilton."

Jennifer turned back to Clint. "Do you think we should move the body? Put it on the rug and cover it with a blanket?"

Clint shook his head. "I think the police would prefer it stay right where it is, at least for now."

Jennifer nodded. A steel gaze came in her eyes. She looked at Ramsey, who almost flinched. Then he shook slightly as if dealing with the aftermath of a panic attack.

"Mr. Ramsey, I am the owner of this Lodge and obviously I am very upset someone used it as a place for murder. So I trust you won't mind if I ask you a few questions - just to aid the police, of course."

Ramsey swallowed, or tried to. It looked like a rock had lodged in his throat. "Of course not. I...I do will anything I can to help," he said.

"Six single individuals checked into my lodge last night. That's a little unusual. I was commenting on that to Clint just last night. Now it turns out that you knew the deceased. Do you know the other four people who checked in?"

"Yes...I...yes."

There was a pause and Jennifer noted the look of sadness in his eyes.

"I realize you are upset, Mr. Ramsey, so just relax and take your time."

"We are all members of the Centennial Historical Society. All of us are history buffs," he finally answered.

"Why did you all check in here?"

Ramsey shifted in his chair. "This may sound unbelievable."

"Let's try it and see," Jennifer said.

"About a hundred and twenty-five years ago there was a Wells Fargo gold shipment in these parts. An outlaw gang headed by a man nicknamed The Falcon stole it. He got the name because he liked heights and the Rocky Mountains and had actually trained a falcon at one time. Rumor is, the gang got about a hundred thousand worth in gold, coins and bars. What's known is the gang drifted apart and a few members got shot, but the gold was never found. We believe it's buried very close by, up in the Rocky Mountain National Forest."

Jennifer nodded. The entrance to the forest was less than five miles from Aspen Breeze. All drivers had to do was turn left when they left the lodge and they would hit the entrance in about ten minutes.

"The Rocky Mountain National Forest is a huge area, thousands of miles there of virtually unexplored wilderness. You better have a specific location or you'll spend your lifetime looking and never find anything," she said.

'We have researched this gang for years. We think we know approximately where the gold was buried. It's more than just recovering the gold. This would be a historical find of enormous significance. We were going up there today to try to find the site."

"Maybe someone didn't want to share," Clint said.

Ramsey shook his head. "I doubt it. I've known these people for years. I don't think anyone would kill Bill. Besides, whoever it was would have to kill all of us too if he wanted to keep the gold to himself. Bill was in the high tech field, lower management, but he also liked the wilderness. He knew this forest better than any of us. We were counting on him to help find the site of the gold. He had searched the forest a number of times during the past five years.

I came out with him a few times. He thought he knew where the outlaws had hid their stash. He shared his opinions with us, but he was the one with the most expertise. Eddie, Eddie Tercelli, one of our group, is the second most knowledgeable about the location. He was out a few times too with Bill searching. But it would be tough for him to find the place on his own."

A blue light waved and flickered in the room. They heard a car door open and then slam shut. They looked up as the officer walked in. He wore a fine, crisp blue uniform with a bright silver badge. He had a slight paunch over his belt, but it didn't make him look old or slow. The intense gray eyes under the rim of the black police cap took in everything. His revolver was clearly visible on his right hip.

"Chief Sandish," Clint said, nodding.

Thanks for reading a sample of my first book, *Murder in the Mountains*. I really hope you liked it.

It will be available on Amazon in April, 2016.

Miles Lancaster

Made in the USA
Middletown, DE
23 September 2016